MARIE-SABINE ROGER

GET WELL
SOON

Translated from the French
by Frank Wynne

PUSHKIN PRESS
LONDON

Pushkin Press
71–75 Shelton Street,
London WC2H 9JQ

Original text © Editions du Rouergue, 2012
Translation © Frank Wynne 2017

First published in French as *Bon Rétablissement* in 2012
This translation first published by Pushkin Press in 2017

1 3 5 7 9 8 6 4 2

ISBN 978 1 782272 16 8

Set in Monotype Baskerville by Tetragon, London
Printed in Great Britain by the CPI Group, UK

www.pushkinpress.com

GET WELL
SOON

I DON'T LIKE to big myself up, but by the time I was, maybe, six or seven, I'd already had a crack at a bunch of things in terms of committing crimes and stuff that's illegal by law. Aggravated robbery, sexual assault and battery, blackmail and extortion…

The sexual assault and battery involved snogging Marie-José Blanc. She kept her teeth clenched so I didn't exactly get very far. But it's the thought that counts.

I'd commit aggravated robbery every Saturday after rugby: I'd blag sweets and stuff from the littler kids. I'd smack them about a bit in the changing rooms. Sometimes I'd show mercy to one of them. I've got a bit of Robin Hood in me.

If you want to know about the extortion, just ask my brother. He used me as a bad example with his kids when they were young. Don't grow up like your uncle, or you'll have me to deal with. In my defence, I have to say that if he had nothing to be ashamed of, he wouldn't have emptied his piggy bank and handed me the cash. To guilt-trip someone, they have to be guilty.

People called me "The Terror." I thought that was pretty cool! I felt like I was destined for greatness.

Back then, there were five and a bit of us living at home: my parents, my kid brother and me, *pépé* Jean and my dead *mémé* Ginou.

My paternal grandparents had died in a dumb accident when my father was only eight, refusing to give way, it was my grandmother's fault, she never saw the point of stop signs.

My father was brought up by his grandparents, his mother's parents: *pépé* Jean, still very much alive and kicking at the time I'm talking about, and *mémé* Ginou in her cremation urn out in the garage.

I found it difficult to imagine how he must have felt, heading back to school the day of the accident, when he realized his folks were never coming home again. At the time, he could have thought he was finally free to live his life: no more bare-arse whipping for every little slip-up. Freedom.

Total freedom.

But listening to him talk about his childhood, I could tell that there are some kinds of freedom which fuck up your life more surely than a whole bunch of restrictions. Based on that, it didn't seem all that tempting, getting to be an orphan. I was quite fond of my parents, despite the fact that they were parents, with all the shortcomings that implies authority-wise. I was particularly fond of my father. I thought he was cool, and not just because he had biceps thicker than most people's thighs. He was a strong guy, in every sense. Feet firmly planted in his size elevens. He had no shortage of opinions, though he didn't have much else. He was a bigmouth, a bruiser, but the kind of guy who had to get out the hankies at weddings and christenings and called my mother "my little love bundle" and didn't give a toss if people laughed, and was never afraid to tell her "I love you".

The man I most probably wanted to be.

Even as a little kid, I could tell the power he had over people from the way they would always say to me:

"Oh, your father! Your father... He's really somebody!"

He was so good at being *somebody* that, next to him, I felt like nobody.

Personally, I would have preferred a father who was a bit more ordinary. It would have made it easier to leave the nest.

The worst thing about it was that I was the *eldest*, I was the standard-bearer. My brother brought himself up without bothering anyone, he was blessed. He was the youngest, the second child. The perpetual runner-up in the human race.

I was the one they were pinning their hopes on.

I still remember the way they looked at us, our neighbours, our cousins, and every man jack. The sliding glance from my-father-the-hero to his snot-nosed-shit-stirring-brat. The sad, incredulous faces that silently said:

"How is it even possible? How can a guy like this father a kid like that?"

I probably worked out pretty early that I could never fill my father's boots and in order to survive I'd have to find some different footwear.

I made every effort to be as much of a pain in the arse as possible and the most creative arsehole. Unfortunately, I had no real vices: for all my pretence at being a hoodlum, underneath I was a sweet kid.

I wished I could be a Mafioso, a bad guy, a bastard. Actually, I was an arse-wipe. A two-bit moron with no ambition.

And to top it all, my father would always lay a hand on my shoulder and say:

"He's a complete dunce, but he's a good kid. I'm sure he'll go far anyway…"

That was probably his way of showing he believed in me.

But to my ears *anyway* sounded a lot like a despairing *in spite of everything.*

A LOT OF WATER has flowed under the bridge since then. And if I didn't drown, I'd have to say I came pretty close. A few days ago, I was fished out of the Seine just in the nick of time.

Two feet from the bank, to be precise, but that's more than far enough to sink into the mud and float to the surface a couple of weeks later, limp and soggy as the hunks of bread people throw to the ducks.

They cleared out my bronchial tubes, put various bits of me in plaster. I had clearly ricocheted off the bridge. Botched suicide, drunken binge, mugging? Everyone had a theory.

I was in a coma, so I could hardly voice an opinion.

I woke up in intensive care with multiple trauma, which sounds pretty impressive, watched over by a concerned-looking cop. The sort of kid my father might have spared, even on a day of political unrest. He was a young guy, a decent sort, with huge, sad antelope eyes and a three-day beard he'd probably been growing for three months.

He seemed completely overawed. My charisma, obviously. Or maybe the chest drain, the oxygen mask and all the huge tangle of wires to keep me monitored had something to do with it too.

This junior cop was a young thirty-five, he had a black leather jacket and a black leather notebook with the face of Chewbacca printed on the spine. He could have been my son, if I'd ever procreated.

When I opened my eyes, I did it like a drowning man desperately trying to catch his breath. Then again, I had drowned, or as good as, so that probably explains it.

I wondered what I was doing here, feeling a vague uneasiness over the general anaesthesia and the unpleasant sensation of not knowing where I began and ended. Part of my mind was panicked, racing in every direction, trying to get the lie of the land, where the fuck am I? Am I still in one piece? Can I move?

The other part could not tear itself from the face of this strange guy leaning over me, too close, who was whispering so low that I could hardly hear a thing. The words seemed to come from far away, his voice sounded weird, much too slow.

Eventually, I managed to catch the phrase:

"… any idea what might have happened to you? Because, right now, we've made no progress in our investigation…"

Then, studying the oxygen mask, he added:

"Just a yes or no will do. Do you remember what happened?"

I dimly shook my head, just enough to set the ceiling spinning and the mattress lurching. Sorry. I had no idea how I'd got there.

He asked me another question, one that took some time

to percolate. Before I closed my eyes, I shook my head again. No: I had not tried to put an end to my life.

I've no wish to kill myself.

Time will take care of that bit of business.

ACCORDING TO the latest estimate, I've been here a week. I haven't seen the time passing.

I've felt it, though.

I sleep too much during the day, I'm zonked out by various drugs, by inactivity, everything merges into the same grey monotony, Monday, Tuesday, Wednesday. I don't remember diving into the river, but there's nothing to be done. Don't remember being fished out, or being brought here either.

Apparently they sedated me because I was agitated and distressed. Not distressed in the sense of being upset, I'm never upset when I'm being a pain in the arse to other people.

No, *distressed*, meaning troubled or confused.

They put the kibosh on my ability to think, to move, to hinder the work of the nurses and doctors. On the plus side: I spent a couple of days off my face—the piss-up of the century—feeling like I was waking up every five minutes and sleeping for ten hours at a stretch in between, and I wasn't in too much pain.

I feel a lot worse now. I ache all over.

And when I'm not in pain, I feel like I *am* an ache.

They sliced me open here and there to reset fractures and patch things up. I've got more pins and plates than a middle-class matron. My ID is the pile of X-rays that the doctors—especially the surgeon—pore over with an air of satisfaction: iliac spine, iliac crest, obturator foramen, femoral neck, femur, tibia and fibula.

Moving is out of the question, it's strictly prohibited.

Normally I'm a spinning top, I toss and turn to try and get to sleep, now here I am forced to lie completely still, and, to make matters worse, I'm flat on my back.

It makes nights seem longer than a philosophy lecture.

I'm experiencing life in hospital. I've heard people talk about it, now I know first-hand.

As soon as you're admitted, you want to get up and go home, the way dogs tug on their leads and try to turn back when they arrive at the vet's. I feel like a mangy mutt, tail between my legs, coat dull.

I want my doggy bowl, my blanket, my bone, my basket.

I want to go home.

Besides, I can't stand the smell of hospitals.

They don't smell hygienic, they smell of disinfectant, of cleaning products with phony fragrances to hide the stink of pus and piss, of "little accidents" and other horrors.

They don't smell like home cooking—a nice stew simmering—they smell of canteen grub. Even the coffee doesn't smell right. The aroma slinks along the walls like a traitor in the shadows, seeps into the hallways and the rooms, sneaky, insidious, sinister. Pour it into a cup and its weakness is clear, it's a watery-black, warmed-up cat's piss, deeply disappointing.

As for tea, there's only one choice: stomach-churning chamomile.

The days start early, 6.00 a.m., which leaves lots of time to feel depressed later. The morning duty-nurse swings the door open like a cowboy swaggering into a saloon, flicks on the fluorescent lights that burn my eyes and shouts *Morrrrr-ning!* in a voice too loud for my sleepy ears and, without bothering to find out if I'm awake (which I am, thanks for asking), takes my blood pressure and my temperature.

I'm entitled to two white tablets whose name and purpose are a mystery to me, then she fills out the form hanging at the end of the bed, turns off the incandescent fluorescent then leaves, not closing the door, saying have a nice day without a shred of irony.

Then one of the lady orderlies—always cheery—arrives with breakfast, two cellophane-wrapped *biscottes*, some neurasthenic fruit compote, a tiny jar of jam that's never met a real fruit in its life and a plain yoghurt.

Unfailingly, even if she's seen me a day ago or two days ago, she asks,

"And what would monsieur like this morning?…"

To get out of here, Dear God, to get out!

"… coffee, tea, milk?"

She opens the venetian blinds, fluffs my pillow, sets the tray down just out of reach, forcing me to perform various painful contortions forbidden by my surgeon.

*

Then the day begins, with ten times as many hours as a day spent on the outside.

Through the open door I can see people wandering past, which doesn't bother me, and they can see me, which really bothers me.

I've given up watching telly. I think the programmes are devised by people in high places to free up hospital beds and deal with patients who overstay. Thrilling European cop shows, electrifying game shows and live coverage of the workings of the *Assemblée nationale* can do a lot to speed up the death of old codgers and encourage other patients to rip out their IVs.

The only thing I watch is the news, brilliant as always at focusing on good news—war, pollution, tsunamis, old people getting beaten up by young thugs, childhood depression and smoker's cancer—in a commendable shot at positive thinking.

Or sometimes at night I'll watch a movie, but not often.

The rest of the time, I've got all the time in the world. The direct and demonstrable consequence: I think.

Thinking is a morbid occupation that I prefer to avoid in most cases. Especially given that, since in here there's no escape mechanism, I contemplate my navel, my thoughts frantically spinning like a crazed hamster in its wheel. Me, *me*, my life, my achievements.

Career paths and trajectories, inventory of fixtures.

Status report. Just the phrase makes me want to throw up.

"Status report" smacks of bankruptcy.

*

Lunch is at 11.30 a.m. and the evening meal is at 6.20 p.m.

My room is at the far end of the corridor, so my food is lukewarm or stone-cold and inedible depending on the swiftness of the orderly and the length of her legs. Since most of them are from Madagascar, I get a lot of sympathy and very few calories.

The other day, I asked one of the nurses why they didn't reschedule the meals by a couple of hours. She explained that it was because the night staff are responsible for serving breakfast before they go off shift and "if you changed one thing you'd have to change everything". Fine, I said, in that case the night staff could take over serving dinner from the day staff, who could take over serving breakfast, and, by my reckoning, it wouldn't make any more work for anyone.

Her only response was to stick a thermometer in my ear, a procedure I had some trouble getting used to at first.

THE STAFF CALL ME the "guy fished out of the Seine". News must have been slack, because the local papers ran a few short articles about me.

This was more than enough to give me a vague air of mystery that I'm actively trying to cultivate—though it's too early to tell how successful I've been. In fact, I think it's pretty commendable of me to want to remain enigmatic when I'm reduced to having my arse wiped like a big baby and everyone in the hospital, regardless of title or rank, feels entitled to ask whether I'm having trouble making pee-pee—and everything else—before they even bother saying good morning.

I have to say it is kind of amazing, this kind of relationship. Not a day goes by without someone asking me—with an interest that seems completely sincere—whether I've passed wind this morning. That said, I've got a sense that they wouldn't appreciate it if I responded:

"Yes, thank you, what about you?"

Hold up, now!

Don't go getting above your station.

I'm the patient here.

And it takes a lot of bloody patience to put up with the enforced inactivity, the discomfort of being in plaster, the sweltering heat of the hospital room, the lack of privacy.

Long story short, I'm not feeling myself at the moment. I feel like, as far as everyone else is concerned, I'm just a bladder to be drained, a bowel obstruction, a few fractures and some drains.

Not to mention the strange way they address me:

"And how are we today?"

I have to bite my tongue to stop myself saying:

"*We* are fine, we thank you."

"We" have a surname, a first name, and—in case anyone's interested—a whole slew of births, marriages and deaths:

Jean-Pierre Fabre, widower, childless, retired, born in Perpignan, 4th October 1945—the day Social Security was enacted, which probably explains my constant budget deficit—son of Roger Fabre, railwayman, born 17th November 1922 in Marseille and Odette Augier, unemployed, born 25th June 1924 in Avignon.

It's my pelvis that's cracked.

My head is fine.

THE MORNING AFTER I was admitted, the hospital got in touch with my brother Hervé. Not to try and broker a family reconciliation, just for administrative purposes.

His name and address were in my wallet, and I have to say, I'm still surprised.

A week later, after they had time to get me "moved up to orthopaedic surgery", they finally allowed me visitors—the way they give visitation rights to well-behaved convicts—and I saw him scuttle in, dripping sweat, breathless from the cigarettes, the stress, the stairs. Always been one of life's worriers, my brother. Always fretting about himself, going to pieces for everyone else.

As soon as he saw me, he let out a forlorn "Oh my God!"

I said, "Everything's fine."

He gave me a lukewarm once-over, obviously not very optimistic.

It has to be said that hospital makes you see life from different angles. Angles that are not exactly exciting, like pain, suffering and death, which make most people uncomfortable. Except maybe for pathologists, who probably get so excited they get a hard-on when they furtively sneak into an intensive care unit.

I gestured to the chair.

He sat down and mopped his forehead. At first we said nothing, then, in two sentences, we tackled the circumstances of the accident (I was pretty vague on the details), and the length of my stay here (I didn't really know yet).

So, to take my mind of things, he told me about his marital problems.

My brother and his wife Claudine don't have much in common any more. Like a couple of knackered old dray horses, they're pulling in different directions. He suffers from irritable bowel syndrome because she makes his life shit. She suffers from migraine because he does her head in. What's more, she's going deaf, which will deprive her of the spice of life: the daytime soaps. On the other hand, she won't have to listen to him cough and kvetch. Always, in all things, look for the silver lining.

They remind me of what we were like, Annie and me, even though I did love her before she left me. I know the feeling, know it all too well, the burden of the everyday, the yoke that keeps a couple together, stops you from parting company and probably from falling flat on your face.

Hervé concluded with a sigh:

"You don't know how lucky you are, you've got it cushy here."

He looked at me on my sickbed, suddenly remembered I was widowed and realized what he had just said.

To create a diversion, he talked about his son, who is doing volunteering work with a humanitarian organization in Haiti—we all have our cross to bear—and about my niece and her husband, with whom I've been lucky enough to spend very little time. I've nothing against them, and that pains me. They're polite, small-minded, unimaginative. Honest folk, just like him. I take after my great-grandfather, *pépé* Jean, I have a healthy aversion to family ties and their knotty acolytes. That said—is it age? Have I gone soft?—I have a lot of time for their son Jérémy, my great-nephew, who's a smart, likeable guy. He showed me how to torrent pirated movies, and just for that I have a lot of respect for him.

At the end of the visit, I gave Hervé the keys to my apartment.

"Do you think you could pop round and pick up a couple of things from the house? Just my laptop, my toothbrush and things. And some clothes, if it's not too much trouble."

He's an obliging kind of guy, he brought everything round that same evening.

Since he could not bring himself to leave straight away, he sat for a while, not knowing what to say or do, anxiously reviewing the tubes coming out of various parts of me, though he had made a detailed survey of them this morning.

"I know, I look like a gasworks," I said.

He nodded but said nothing. He went over and stared out of the window at the passageway where patients in pyjamas were probably wheeling their IV stands and bags filled with mysterious fluids. He opened my wardrobe, moved a chair, considered the size of the room, "You're lucky, it's huge, but it's hardly surprising, there are two beds." He glanced at the cramped bathroom as he gave me the sales pitch, as though I were a prospective buyer.

"Pretty swish, isn't it? Washbasin, shower, toilet…"

"As bathrooms go, it's cutting-edge," I said.

"Um, well, yeah. Actually while I'm here, and talking about toilets…"

Later, he pointed out that you could die of heatstroke in a hospital room. They're designed to be warm, I told him, given that most people here—or the patients at least—are usually a little delicate. He nodded.

There was a silence.

He said:

"OK, right, well…"

Conversation between us has been on life support for a long time now.

To save him from floundering, I babbled:

"It's a shame, I completely forgot to ask you to bring me some books!"

"Oh… right, well, I'll pop by your place next week when Claudine and I come to visit. You can give me a list, if you know roughly what you want."

"Whatever you find on the bedside table would be great, thanks."

"Right, well…"

He was probably cursing himself that he did not have the courage to scarper as fast as his legs could carry him. I decided to put him out of his misery. I pretended to stifle a yawn, and said in a feeble voice:

"I hope you don't mind, but I'm feeling a bit peaky. I'm just going to get forty winks."

He jumped at the chance.

"No, sure, of course, you're bound to be tired, it's only normal. Right well… I'll be off then?"

We hugged.

When he got to the door, just before he left, he turned his mournful Saint Bernard eyes on me.

"All the same… You're in a terrible state."

"It looks a lot worse than it is, from what they tell me."

"No chance, you're going to need months of physio."

"Well, maybe not months…"

"Are you kidding me? You don't get over something like this in a couple of weeks, especially not at your age. Right, well, I'll head off and let you get some sleep, you look awful."

I said:

"Thank very much, good to see you."

Deep down, I'm pretty fond of my kid brother really. He's very sweet.

On the other hand, he's very blunt.

EVERY TIME my brother leaves, he leaves me with a guilty conscience, and I hate myself for hating myself. I appreciate his efforts to help out. I'd do the same for him, and he knows that. Family obligations aren't just there for decoration. The only problem is the four years between us meant we were never able to have a real bond. That's life.

Aside from our parents, we have nothing in common.

I was in the big boys' class in primary school by the time he started first year with his fat knees covered in scabs and bruises and his skinny legs in shorts that were miles too big for him. I was off to the lycée by the time he pushed open the gate to secondary school.

To me, he was always *little*.

Little bastard, little toerag, little snitch, little squirt.

Little brother.

The living evidence of my parents' betrayal, since they had seen fit to spawn him without bothering to consult me, even though they already had *me*, and that should have been enough to make them happy.

Who can describe the pain of elder brothers and sisters, forced to share their Carambar, their father's shoulders, their mother's kisses, the back seat of the car, their scooter and their bicycle? Who can describe the frustration of being transformed pretty much overnight and against your will into the one who is supposed to *set a good example*?

But I took the role to heart, Hervé can attest to that. I did everything I could to teach him about life, real life, Chinese burns and back-stabbing and itching powder. Thanks to me, his childhood was one long hazing.

I was the insufferable older brother.

I am the impenetrable old brother.

Given how old we are, I'm afraid it will be that way for life.

I WAS IN THE PROCESS of replying to an email, uncomfortably settled the flat of my back, laptop on the bed tray, screen tilted at a precarious angle, glasses perched on the tip of my nose, looking like an elderly schoolmaster—ironic for someone who was always a dunce—when one of the cleaning operatives, who had been mopping the floor around the bed for at least fifteen minutes, finally said sarcastically:

"Writing your life story?"

I smiled.

I've always found it a strange idea, writing *memoirs*. There's something pathetic about it. Like writing your own funeral eulogy, because you're already bitching that if you want something doing properly, do it yourself. Before exiting the building you polish what you can, dust off everything and sweep the cat shit under the rug.

But, thinking about it, I realized that it was as good a way to pass the time as any.

After all, why not?

So I decided to make an inventory of everything I remember about my life. I'm a methodical guy. I'll recap everything I know. And although the results may be of no interest to anyone—including me, since I'm not remotely sure that I'll want to read what I've written—I set to work.

I even start making notes on the laptop, a sort of intimate personal palaeontology on an Excel spreadsheet. Old habits die hard. A life spent working in logistics leaves its mark.

I've wheedled to be allowed to keep my laptop within easy reach, plugged in and perched on the bed tray I've transformed into a desk. I might bark and roar for someone to close the door, but I can be all sweetness and light if I need to, so I can have the computer close to me.

Necessity is the mother of diplomacy.

D IGGING DOWN through the deepest strata, here I am at the age of six and a bit, when I was obsessed with *scaffles*, the only thing anyone seemed to talk about round our house that year.

I spent a lot of time wondering what it was, this *scaffle* people were constantly banging on about. To be honest, at first, I thought it had something to do with trees. Huge, gnarly trees. The sort of trees where you would find monkeys or panthers.

Or maybe rocky mountaintops, why not?

But after mature reflection, I came to a firm conclusion: scaffles were seafaring boats. Not flat-bottomed boats or riverboats or miserable little dinghies. They were ships. Huge ships. The sort that laugh in the face of squalls and hurricanes, that sneer at the Atlantic, the Pacific and all the seas ending in *–ic* that we call oceans. That mystery being solved, the only thing on my mind was to find out which port they sailed from. And whether they would take me, whether they would want me. But *that*, in the end, was something I would make my business. I was always making everything my business.

I was six years old, I had all my baby teeth, I knew about life.

They'd take me on, I was sure of it.

Besides, they were probably warships, given the devastating effect the mere mention of them had in the living room. My mother would let out a wail and touch wood—it had to be round and unvarnished, so usually a chair leg. My father would turn purple and hiss in a demented voice from high in his throat:

"Bloody hell, I don't believe it!"

It was always triggered by nothing at all, or nothing very much.

And it was always triggered by pépé Jean.

Pépé Jean, my great-grandfather, who spent his life sitting by the window in his leather armchair that stank of beer because of the shakes, and from here he could see half the clock, three-quarters of the street and the whole of my parents when they were sitting at the table. Pépé Jean, who listened in religious silence to *Signé Furax* every day, just after one o'clock, on the huge Pathé 507 radio.

My pépé, an iron fist in an abrasive glove.

I was by far his favourite subject. He liked to broach it mid-afternoon. He would clear his throat, give a little cough, huh-hem!—the meeting is now in session—then start mumbling to himself.

"What are you going on about, pépé?" my father would say after about five minutes, not bothering to look up from his crossword.

Pépé Jean would suck in a lungful of air, enough to make

31

it to the end of his sentence, and answer fitfully because he often stalled mid-word.

"That youn-gster of yours is a little repr-robate!"

"Oh, give over, pépé…" my father would sigh.

"I kn-ow you don't want to lis-sten, but that child is a little mo-onster!"

He would stare at me with black beady eyes that oozed like those of a dog with mange, and his tongue snaked out to slide his false teeth back into place. I would pull hideous faces at him, keeping my back to my parents, for whom respect for one's elders was sacrosanct and a clip round the ear the surest way to ensure it was observed.

Waving his walking stick at me menacingly, Pépé would conclude:

"Ma-ark my wo-ords, you'll wi- wind up climbing the sca-scaff-fold!"

My father would twist his napkin or toss it on the table.

Sometimes he would angrily snap one of the pencils with a rubber on the end.

My mother swore that this kind of talk would bring bad luck.

I could see why she was worried: the thought of watching me climb aboard one of these scaffles where real men like me enlisted to fight wars and kill enemies must have scared her. She feared for my life.

Pretty standard, for a mother.

Unfortunately, my father would always give a loud, cruel laugh and say:

"Don't you worry your pretty head, love. Your son's not going to wind up on the scaffold! Of course he won't. No danger."

He had no faith in me.

And that, now *that* is really tough for a kid.

T HE INSPECTOR always knocks politely, even when the door is open, which is most of the time. He comes in, says hello and asks:

"Not disturbing you, am I?"

If I tell him I was just about to pop out, he laughs.

I don't think he is making much headway in his investigation. Or at least, he doesn't talk about it.

He talks about the weather, about what I'm reading. About me writing *my memoirs*. He's fascinated that I'm constantly tapping on my laptop.

But *why* he comes, I don't know.

His name is Maxime. He mentioned his surname only to immediately dismiss it:

"Call me Maxime."

"You could call me Chateaubriand—seeing as I'm hard at work on my *Memoirs from Beyond the Grave*," I said, "Otherwise I'll settle for Jean-Pierre."

He laughs. He knows his memoirists. But he elects to call me Monsieur Fabre. I don't complain.

A little deference does no harm in relations, whether personal or police-related.

I suspect he feels sorry for me and is only visiting the

train wreck in Room 28 out of pity when he's got a spare moment, or has a case to deal with nearby.

Either that or he's bored.

Or he's trying to pick up one of the nurses in white coats. Rumour has it they wear nothing underneath.

I've craned my neck so hard I have nearly given myself a herniated disc, but I haven't seen anything to substantiate this rumour.

Patience.

I've noticed that his presence at my bedside has brought colour to the cheeks of the nursing aides. I'm hoping to get some small benefit from it, maybe their fondness for him will rub off on me. They seem to think he's cute, this weirdo with his brooding good looks. No sooner does he arrive than they start coming and going outside my door pretending to act natural. When he leaves, they probably follow him down the corridor like a shoal of cod.

I'm well aware that the old codger swaddled in bandages like a silkworm's cocoon doesn't set their pulses racing like that.

It doesn't matter, if his visits to my room get me an extra ration of plonk at mealtimes, it's better than nothing. I'm not expecting any incidental pleasures, I'm a realist.

Hope is fine for dreamers and adolescents. Me, I've got memories.

At my age, it's a better bet than having ambitions.

This morning, he's got a glint in his eye.

"Monsieur Fabre, I've got news for you!"

"I'm listening, my young friend."

I like calling him that. At first he found it disconcerting, but now, bizarrely, I think it makes him feel at ease.

He pulls a chair up to the bed, sits down, leans over me and looks deeply into my eyes. It seems he's about to drop a bombshell and is trying to use his huge dark eyes to send a subliminal message to warn me in advance.

I'm polite, I show an interest.

"Come on then, tell me all."

"The investigation has concluded it was an accident."

He draws back to gauge the effect.

When it seems clear that I suspected as much, he looks disappointed and continues:

"Caused by a motorist."

"…"

"A hit-and-run driver!"

I can see he's doing his best to please the customer. I feel sorry for him, so I raise an eyebrow.

"Do you have any details?"

His face lights up and he enthusiastically launches into an explanation.

"Well, now you come to mention it, we do: the evidence suggests you were rammed by a car whose driver lost control of the vehicle."

I was fairly sure it wasn't a Mafia hit: the only Mafiosi I see regularly are those in *The Godfather* and *Donnie Brasco*.

He takes out his Star Wars-style tablet and sketches

something quickly, biting his lower lip as he mutters a running commentary.

"OK, so here… here's the bridge… You must have been standing on the pavement… I'd say… ummmm… somewhere about here. You see?"

It's obvious that he enjoys this, drawing maps, cutaway diagrams, perspectives with vanishing points with little arrows and crosses. He probably dreamt of being an architect, but his father was a civil servant. The sort of tragedy you come across every day.

"So, what we think—well, our *hypothesis*—is that you were thrown over the parapet, at, let's say, this sort of angle… there… like *thaaat*… see?"

"Gosh."

"Yep. It must have been a violent collision, given the fractures you suffered."

"Let me get this right, you're saying it's a miracle that I'm still here…"

He nods.

"Too right. And given the time—this time of year at five in the morning there's not much traffic, right? Were you coming home from a night out with friends?"

"I doubt it. I don't have any."

He shoots me a sympathetic look, coughs, gives an embarrassed smile and changes the subject.

"Well, whatever the situation, the fact remains that were it not for the person standing under the bridge, you wouldn't be here now…"

The "person" in question was the young rent boy who pulled me out of the river. He witnessed the dive. He didn't know how to swim, but seeing as I did a belly-flop and landed near the bank, he managed to snag me with a boat hook and pull me to the edge. Alerted by his shouts, the bin men on the opposite bank called the emergency services. The young guy kept my head out of water until the paramedics arrived.

The doctors told me that if he had tried to haul me up onto the jetty, he would have completely dislocated my pelvis.

Smashed up in an accident, half drowned in the Seine, saved by a rent boy and a bunch of dustmen.

I'll say one thing, it never gets boring: my destiny is the gift that just keeps on giving.

T HE GOOD THING about hospitals is their total respect for your personal space.

I've already asked the nurses and the aides a hundred times to close the door when they leave the room. When I'm awake I have no trouble enforcing my wishes: I inherited my father's voice. But if I should nod off, I wake up to find the door open—wide open, half open or slightly ajar, depending on the laziness of whoever was last to leave, or the level of animosity they feel towards me.

That said, in general, the people here are reasonably discreet. Mostly, they just pop their heads round the door and when they see me on my sickbed hammering away on the laptop, or snoring noisily, or taking zero pleasure eating a meal that has zero flavour, they turn away out of a sense of propriety. They leave me to it.

All except the snot-nosed brat.

A short, tubby girl with terrible hair who's thirteen, maybe fourteen, I'm no expert in spotty teenagers. Ever since they moved me up to orthopaedic surgery, I feel like I see her at least ten times a day. And every time she gives me this strange look. I can't help wondering what the hell she's doing on this ward. No plaster cast, no crutches, no walking frame. No sign of an arm in a sling or even a minor limp. Just a sizeable excess of flab that accentuates her bulldog charm.

Today, like most days, I find myself exposed to the prying eyes of anyone walking around the corridors. And then she shows up again. She slows down, stares at me. Takes her time.

If I gave in to my baser instincts, I'd lift the sheet and give her a quick flash of my balls—I can't flash my arse since I'm flat on my back. But given her age, I worry people might get the wrong impression. I'm no paedophile. And then there are aesthetic considerations: they've catheterized my pocket rocket because I suffered urethral trauma, so what with the oedema in my bollocks, I look like I've had a set of bagpipes grafted onto me.

In any case, flashing the family jewels would just be a creative way of letting her know she's busting my balls, constantly coming round to check out the décor and stare at me, freshly plastered and nailed to the bed.

There's probably not much in the way of entertainment, I can understand that, but I'm not some unpaid clown, I just want everyone to bugger off and leave me alone.

T HE ADVANTAGE of being a childless widower is that
you're not mobbed by visitors.

Not that this seems to stop people popping in and out as
though the place has a revolving door: honestly, I haven't
seen so many people in years. Only people involved in caring
for me. Nurses, auxiliaries, doctors of various kinds and—
the God among Gods in this white-coated Olympus—my
surgeon, who is my favourite.

He's a gruff little man with an icy stare who talks at me as he
scans the patient file and makes all the nurses jumpy as fleas.

He is precise, concise. Maybe it's the fact that he spends
his time cutting away the superfluous, but in conversation
he sticks to the basics. And even then, he's unforthcoming.
He speaks in simple sentences: subject-verb-object. On his
very first visit, he reeled off an inventory of my injuries in a
tone that sounded as though he were bored rigid.

Pelvic fracture: stable.

Fractures of tibia and fibula, reduced: metal plate here,
two screw fixations there.

I felt like a horse with a farrier examining his shoes.

Then he graced me with a forced smile as he explained
that—in the end—I had not required arthrodesis. He was so

obviously piqued at not being able to perform this procedure that I did not dare ask what it meant. I just gave him a cha-grined smile and resolved to Google "arthrodesis" as soon as he left. It is a surgical procedure that entails *permanently fusing the bones of a joint.* I feel bad for disappointing him.

Since then, I see him Tuesdays and Thursdays, late in the morning.

According to his latest status report, hot off the press this morning (always assuming I understood it correctly): I'm doing well—everything is going well—he's happy—I'm happy that he's happy.

He is pleased with me (translation: with his results).

In two to three weeks I will be able to start walking with crutches, and gradually putting weight on my left foot. If there are no complications.

Not that there's any reason to assume there will be.

Although…

For the time being, however, I have to lie flat on my back.

In four or five days, a nurse will come to *elevate me thirty degrees.* I almost said that was more than I could hope for, at my age. But I bit my tongue. No need to risk reprisals for my pathetic sense of humour.

Although…

Finally, with a harried air, as though eager to be done with me, he said:

"Any questions, Monsieur Fabre?"

"No… No, thank you, but for now, I don't see wh—"

"… in that case everything's perfect!"

Perfect.
There you go.
Perfect.
Just the word I was looking for.

I'M HOPING to carry on with this occupation of mine, this writing. Though it would be helpful if things came back to me in order. But memory is a weathervane, the slightest breeze sets it spinning.

A little while ago, on the news, a weary worker was being interviewed by a reporter outside the gates of a striking factory. She was fifty-something, her delicate features just beginning to fade, her face was drawn, her eyes pale, she had a look of quiet dignity and that bitter little crease at the corner of the lips carved by a lifetime of constant setbacks.

She looked just as I remember Annie.

Ever since, I've been thinking about her.

I met Annie when I was twenty-six. She was cheerful, loving and five years younger than me. I found her beautiful, she found me handsome, sound reasons to keep her for yours truly. We married six months later, and we were together for thirty-one years, until her accident. Falling from a bike on wet cobblestones on her way to the post office. What people call a senseless way to die.

I don't know any sensible ways.

She was fifty-two, I was fifty-seven. We'd tried our best to have kids, her and me, but nothing doing. Or nothing that would bring them to term. After the third miscarriage, Annie gave up. The difference between us was that I never had a child, whereas she had carried three.

I don't know whether it's about something to do with being a man, a moron, or both, but I've never considered a foetus to be a child in its own right. I was barely getting to grips with the difference it might make to my life when it was all over.

Nothing had moved in my belly. She had felt the tentative little stirrings.

Annie lost her babies around the fourth month. I was sad, obviously, but I wasn't devastated. The first time, I think I might even have felt a bit relieved for a minute. I was scared of the idea of a baby coming between us. I was scared of losing my freedom, of no longer being able to do exactly what I wanted. I was a selfish, immature arsehole.

These are the terrible things you can finally face up to when you're pushing sixty. You've nothing left to hide any more. You've learnt not to judge yourself too harshly.

But I remember, a few years later, being horrified that I could ever have thought such a thing.

After the first miscarriage, I tried to console her, saying: "It'll be fine next time."

After the second, I didn't know what to say to her. I listened to her sobbing in the bathroom for nights on end, not daring to say anything, afraid that I wouldn't be able to find the right words.

I would have been better off saying something, even if it meant saying something dumb. A sincere mistake is easier to forgive than a comfortable silence. It is more quickly forgotten, too.

Annie visited every specialist possible, the one with bronze plaques on well-heeled, tree-lined avenues, with art prints and potted plants, even those specialists whose fees were not covered by the *Sécurité sociale*. She consulted psychics, gurus, magnetic healers; she had healing crystals laid on her belly, chakras unblocked, needles jabbed along her meridians; she had blood tests, X-rays, ultrasounds; she intoned mantras; she swallowed pills, gel capsules, and promises that, as everyone knows, are binding only for those who believe.

Over a period of seven or eight years she spent a fortune in time, in money, in vain hope, in shattered dreams. A thousand times she was told that she had to hope, that hope would keep her alive.

Hope mostly keeps alive those who profit from it.

I HAVE BEEN very lucky: I love my job.

My *jobs* would be more exact, since I have held various different positions.

The six-year-old who desperately longed to go aboard a scaffle ended up spending thirty-five years working in the merchant navy. I've seen my fair share of freighters, ferries, tankers, cargo ships of every kind, grain, coal, cement and mineral ore. Each time I signed up was an adventure, each time I docked in France a well-deserved rest, a welcome respite, just as long as it did not last too long.

I can't help it, I've got a workhorse mentality, I need to pull my plough, to sweat and toil to feel alive. I need fresh air, wide open spaces. And something to keep me busy.

Three weeks at home, and I would be standing at the window, pawing the ground, or out in the garden, hocks tensed, wild-eyed, nostrils flaring in the breeze.

"I can tell you're bored stiff," Annie would say.

And immediately afterwards:

"When do you ship out again?"

M ORNINGS ARE pretty dismal. I don't sleep much.
Too uncomfortable.

That, and a touch of depression at the thought that I'll have
to stay here for at least another month, *if there are no complications. Not that there's any reason to assume there will be. Although…*

They reassure me with caring voices as though talking
to a child. Now, now, we need to be a patient. Monsieur is
comfortable here, isn't he.

Nope. No, no, no. "Monsieur" is not remotely comfortable, if you want to know.

During the day, I'm bored shitless. At night it's worse.
There are noises in the corridors, nurses laughing and joking,
alarms going off and a background hum of television sets.
Then, everything melds into an oppressive silence punctuated
by phlegmy coughs and muffled whimpers.

The plaster cast makes it almost impossible to sleep. I'm
too hot, the dank sheets cling to me.

Pains constantly breed and multiply, not just mine but
those of every other patient. They burrow inside me, or
spread their wings to invade the adjoining wards, bloodthirsty
vampires fluttering in the darkness.

Aches and pains come in an astonishing variety of forms;
the hospital supplies them wholesale or retail. There are those

that gnaw and those that stab, those that constrict and those that crush. There is the piercing pain that will not let you be, the creeping pain that stealthily grows, silently setting up its equipment before exploding in a wail of bass drums and brass. There is the pain that throbs in your fingertips. The one that has you doubled over in agony. There are those that come armed like the Inquisition, here an axe, there a saw, *hold the knife for me, I'll just grab the pincers.*

There are the vicious pains that wake you in the middle of the night and stay with you until daybreak. The nagging aches in the bones. There is the familiar pain that has been coming and going for so long you greet it like a regular guest: the table set, the bed made up. There are those that invariably turn up with a friend, trailing bouts of nausea, breathlessness, a feeling of suffocation, dizziness, shudders.

There are those that arrive with the fanfare and fireworks of Bastille Day, a tumultuous commotion coursing through the body, and damp squibs in the belly and the stomach. There are the heavy pains, like a cannonball dropped from the fourth floor. The brutal twinges that wrench you apart. The vicious little pains that play the innocent but wreak havoc with your nerves. They drill through you, set your teeth on edge, buzzing inside you like a blowfly circling your head.

After a certain point, a certain threshold, you are merely a body in pain.

There are no thoughts, no patience, no desire to laugh.

When you are truly in pain, you no longer even have a place where you can seek refuge.

You are a territory under enemy control.

I AM PSYCHOLOGICALLY preparing myself to make a start on my meal when there is a knock at the door. This is a sufficiently unusual event that it piques my interest and I look up.

In the doorway stands a pretty creature with a tight-fitting sweater, shoulder-length hair, a slim figure and undulating hips. In a mellifluous voice she asks if she can come in, and I give her a studied growl, "Yesss". She has to come quite close before I realize my mistake. The back-lighting and my traitorous myopia are to blame. The sylph is a boy.

The light in my eyes goes out.

He bats his eyelids hard enough to flutter the sheets and, cooing like a dove, he asks:

"Are you the gentleman who fell into the Seine?"

I reply in a distant tone, priggish and reserved.

"The very same. To whom do I have the honour of speaking?"

"My name is Camille. I was the one who fished you out, I don't know if they told you…"

Oh, so this is my handsome saviour! I give him a broad smile.

He carries on, polite, a little shy.

"I just came to see how you are. But I can see I'm disturbing you, you were about to have lunch…"

On the rectangular plastic tray is a feast for the taste buds: limp beetroot, grey minced beef, soggy cauliflower, a custard tart devoid of soul and of custard.

"The banquet can wait…" I say.

I gesture for him to sit, and he perches one buttock on the chair.

"So, from what I've heard, I owe you my life?"

He mutters No, no, no. I whisper Yes, yes, yes.

He relaxes a little. I continue:

"To tell you the truth, I don't remember anything, it's a complete blank. So, could you tell me what happened?"

This is just what he was waiting for.

He tells me he heard a brutal shriek of brakes up on the bridge, and immediately afterwards he saw me drop into the water like a stone. Fortunately, there was a boat hook lying on the jetty, so he was able to harpoon my parka and drag me to the bank.

"You gave me such a fright! You were so pale and your eyes had rolled back in your head, I really thought you were dead."

I can tell he is still in shock. I try to imagine myself floating on the surface of the water like a huge jellyfish, drifting with the current, white as a Pierrot clown.

Which reminds me, in my family they called me Pierrot, or sometimes Pierrot Gourmand—after the lollipops I consumed by the boxful—a nickname I was stuck with until

I finally left home. Adults can be so sensitive, sometimes, when it comes to kids.

Little Camille gazes at me with a tender, maternal air. He seems to like me. We tend to like people we have helped.

He seems nice, he has an eager look about him, his gestures are graceful, feminine, his face round and his eyes blue as the sky. High cheekbones. Dazzling white teeth—though they're a little crooked. How old is he, this boy? Not even old enough to vote, possibly.

When I was a teenager, there were boys like him in the neighbourhood. A blond lad with a bubble butt whose parents had had the brilliant idea of naming him Jean-Marc, the sort of butch French name that is tough to pull off when you like borrowing your mum's dresses and singing François Deguelt in a shrill soprano.

He got called every name under the sun. Fairy, bumboy, pansy and poof were among the most urbane and flattering.

His father was a truck driver who beat him every Sunday to cure him of his inclinations. His mother would comfort him and call him "my little baby". He was mercilessly teased by every arsehole my age.

His life was a bile sandwich on mouldy bread.

After one weekend that proved too long, he threw himself off the roof of his house. No doubt disillusioned by the sheer magnitude of human stupidity. He botched the high dive and ended up paraplegic.

He had just turned fifteen.

When I found out what happened, I felt shitty, even though I wasn't personally responsible—or no more personally than anyone else. I had never even spoken to him. But I think maybe sidelong glances, sniggers and winks can just as surely push someone over the edge. So, there were a bunch of us who pushed him off the roof that night. His father, first and foremost, with the rest of us cheering him on. All of us, the real men.

By the time you get to my age, unless you've understood nothing at all about life, you don't give a shit about other people's choices. Some people are straight, some people are gay. Some people have multiple loyalty cards. Some are undecided. We don't get to choose what makes us horny any more than we get to choose to be left-handed, or to have curly hair or green eyes.

No merit, no shame.

But with young Camille, the issue isn't being gay. He's a prostitute, that's very different. And he's only a kid, with doe eyes and downy cheeks.

He should be making the most of life, snogging his boyfriend, shopping at the local Ikea to furnish their studio flat instead of turning tricks under a bridge looking like a star pupil dressed up as Slutty Barbie at some Christmas charity bazaar.

Camille goes on talking about my rescue with a wealth of details. I can tell that he's proud. In my opinion, he's got good reason to be. And I can't help thinking that if he hadn't been on the game that night, I would be floating like a turd in the Seine.

His story has a happy ending: the rescuer rescues me, the paramedics paramedic me, and the hero (that's me) is fished out in time. I smile, he smiles too.

Eventually, since we have nothing left to say to each other than "thank you/don't mention it", he gets up, rearranges his fringe and his cotton friendship bracelets.

He mutters:

"Well, I'll leave you to it. I'm really happy to see that you're on the mend."

We shake hands. He heads for the door.

And it is at this point, with the consummate timing I'm famous for, that I ask:

"Is it true you're a rent boy?"

He turns around. I can see in his eyes that I have just ruined something. The elderly Moses, saved from the waters, is nothing more than a dirty old man, a sucker. A john.

Camille comes back over to the bed, his eyes now vacant. It occurs to me that in two seconds he's going to reel off his price list. Given the state of me, the choices would inevitably be limited: a quick wank. I clutch the sheets like a virgin on her wedding night.

But no, he simply stares at me in silence.

I ask:

"How old are you, kid?"

"Twenty-two. Why?"

His tone is edgy, suspicious.

I suddenly realize that, to cap it all, and for no particular reason, I've just called him *kid*, which sounds paternalistic or *Police nationale*, depending on age and criminal record.

"Listen, I don't give a shit who you sell your arse to. But why do you do it?"

He bites his lower lip.

"You don't seem stupid, in fact quite the contrary."

"So?"

"So being a hustler for every lowlife in the area doesn't seem like a job with much in the way of prospects."

I can tell he is getting more and more annoyed. Which is hardly surprising.

"Look, I'm sorry," I stammer, "I'm not exactly subtle, as you might have noticed."

"…"

"And I am *very* grateful, OK?"

I am talking louder and louder. The way things are going, in a couple of minutes I'll be bawling him out. I take a deep breath.

"I owe you my life, and that's a big deal. If you hadn't been there, I'd be dead now. I wouldn't be experiencing the joys of hospital food. You've got to admit, that would have been a terrible shame."

I'm in a hole and I'm still digging, it's pathetic.

"… It's just… I don't know… if I had a kid, it would kill me to know he was doing what you're doing. You get me?"

He doesn't move. He doesn't say anything.

And I am beginning to wonder exactly where I'm going with my lame speech, like a good father who's just worked out that prostitution is not the ideal career path.

He must be intrigued, too; eventually he says in a feeble, disillusioned voice:

"Why are you saying these things? What have you got against me?"

"… Nothing, I don't know, forget it, I'm being stupid. All I want to say is thank you. Sincerely."

He gives me a contemptuous look, then leaves without another word.

The mince is cold. I'm not hungry any more.

Pass me a spade and I'll bury myself.

Hey, mate, I hear you're in hospital? I was wondering why I hadn't heard from you lately. I'm in Brittany for another month or thereabouts, but I'll come visit when I get back.

You can tell me all about it.

Hi! Not much to tell, it's a complete blank—well, almost. I'm up for a visit, I've still got a few spaces in my diary. Meet in Room 28, second floor, I'll be the one sprawled half naked on the little bed, you can't miss me.

What the hell are you doing in Brittany?

On holidays, with Nathalie. It's her niece's wedding tomorrow. 300 guests, absolute madness. We've already been stuffing ourselves like pigs for the past two days. You ever eaten kouign-amann? It's like butter and sugar but with more butter and more sugar, but what's worse is it's like a drug, you can't imagine how addictive this stuff is.

I'll bring you some. At least that way you'll know what you're dying of.

Arsehole

What are you reading at the moment? I'm rereading Duby's *A History of France from its Origins to the Present Day.*

Well played, good choice. Given all the time I've got on my hands, I've started reading the telephone directory. I've just got to "Giraudin, Jean Claude, 13 rue Amiral Courbet".

Oh, yeah, I remember that bit... You'll see, when you get to "Lefebvre, Jocelyne", it starts to get really heartbreaking.

No spoilers! I don't want to know how it ends.

OK, I won't say any more.
　　Behave yourself with the nurses. (Are they obliging?)

When you say "obliging", I assume you're referring to their selfless devotion?

Of course. What else?

I find them pretty obliging, as it goes.

Lucky bastard.

A COUPLE OF MONTHS ago, thanks to Mates of Yesteryear or Buddies from Back in the Day or one of those archaeological websites that shovel nostalgia like manure all over the Internet, I stumbled on my old friend Serge.

Full-time hedonist. Crazy bastard, great lover, insensitive git, forever juggling two women, two break-ups, two disasters. He got in touch with me in early August. Since then, we exchange emails, chat on MSN, talk about books, cooking, old war wounds which in our case means our childhood.

Last time we saw each other was July 1970, in a roadside café somewhere between Bordeaux and Lille. He was handsome as Steve McQueen back when he was playing Josh Randall, I was massacring Dick Rivers' songs on the guitar. I was twenty-five, he was twenty-six. He had a red VW Microbus, I had a beat-up blue Renault Dauphine. We dressed like 'Les Chats Sauvages' or 'Les Chaussettes Noires': black leather jackets, drainpipe trousers, winkle-picker boots. The student riots of May '68 had come and gone without shaking our convictions, we'd rather have died than join the "Peace & Love" brigade, smoking spliffs or growing our hair long. Bell-bottoms and paisley shirts were for chicks. We wore our shirts black and tight across the chest. The fuckwits of the Woodstock generation greeted us with middle and index fingers raised in the V-for-victory, hippy-dippy Peace salute. We returned their salute. Leaving out the index finger, for simplicity's sake.

We thought we were rebels. Everyone else thought we were losers.

Serge had just got a job as a wine rep. I had just started working for an import-export company in the food-processing industry. We had our whole lives ahead of us.

By the time we first met up again, at *La Comète* brasserie, our whole lives were pretty much behind us, and it had happened without our noticing.

He had brought photos from back in the day. Those little Polaroid snaps—the yellowish-brown image, the grey back, the white borders—of such truly shitty quality that they're impossible to digitally scan.

As soon as I stepped into the brasserie, I recognized him, despite the fact that forty-two years had flowed under the bridge. People change, but they don't really change. We still have much the same mug we had as kids. No matter what we do, we preserve a certain family resemblance as we grow old.

He wasn't as bald as me, I wasn't as potbellied as him. I wasn't wearing a guitar slung over my shoulder any more. The music world hadn't missed much.

My friend Serge looked like the Belgian singer Arno, hair tousled, bags big as suitcases under those hangdog eyes, but well upholstered. It was obvious that he'd taken his job in the wine trade to heart. But I know the guy, he's scrupulous. Now there's a rare quality!

What is there to say about yourself when you meet up with someone after so long? Marriage? Kids? In my case, we'd be done and dusted pretty quickly. No children. Widower for the past ten years. No official partner, no casual girlfriend.

And, yeah, maybe you feel a bit lonely, but no one's nagging you…

Serge, that old goat, has been married for thirty-five years to the same woman. Nathalie her name is, small, skinny, blonde, with eyes like a wary cat and utterly faithful.

In a recent photo, they were flanked by two tall, smiling thirty-somethings who were the spitting image of the parents.

"That's the family…"

He seemed happy.

We embroidered a bit on the subject of work, both being happily retired.

Serge was a rep for the same wine merchant for thirty-five years. He had started out unloading barrels and ended up a supervisor; I had moved between companies a couple of times, but always in the merchant navy.

He had spent most of his life with his nose in a wine bottle, I spent mine on the loading docks.

He had travelled from vineyard to vineyard, from *crus classés* to *crus bourgeois*, while I had worked in various commercial ports from the Mediterranean to the Indian Ocean, from the Aegean to the Black Sea.

He had rumpled the sheets of a thousand Campanile, Ibis and sundry Kyriad hotels.

I had spent my nights sweltering under rotating fans in port hotels that smelt of fried food, diesel oil, stale sweat and tobacco smoke, protected from mosquitoes and cockroaches by threadbare mosquito nets.

Our ears had been christened at very different altars. For him, the festive sound of popping corks, the sensual glug-glug. For me, hysterics, shrieking gulls and an engine's roar. He talked to me about vinification, malolactic fermentation, settling. I talked about gantry cranes, stabilizers and side loaders.

We were like kids: we were comparing marbles.

At the end of the jousting match, he nodded in amazement and delight, as though he were proud of me.

You're a real globetrotter, man!

And adventurer, I think you mean.

We laughed all night like teenage boys, our minds keen and our hearts light. We no longer felt our wrinkles, we had a full head of hair with not a single grey, and our paunches were washboard abs.

We had just turned twenty.

A N EVOLUTIONARY miracle: the little lardball can talk. This morning she stopped in the doorway and said: "Hey, m'sieur?!"

I gave her a hostile glare.

"Can I borrow the laptop?"

Not so much as a bloody "hello".

I love this kind of human interaction, it immediately makes me conciliatory. In passing, I noted that she had said *the laptop*, not *your* laptop. Maybe she thought it was provided by the hospital, first come first served. I hesitated between a number of different responses: In your dreams, tubby— Get stuffed—or even "*What else?*"—if only to practise my English conversation.

I said:

"Sorry, I'm using it."

She gave a little shrug that clearly meant my opinion didn't matter. She said offhandedly:

"Yeah, but I *need* to get on Facebook, like, *now*."

"No."

She gave a sigh, as though I were a difficult child refusing to see reason, then she stood there, shifting her weight from one foot to the other, probably expecting me to change my mind.

I was toying with the formulation I might use to tell her to fuck off—euphemistically, of course, given her age—when the nurse appeared with a broad smile pushing a trolley and said in a sing-song voice:

"Time for your bed-baaaath!"

She pushed the door closed on the girl, telling her in the same perky tone.

"Why don't you come back later, OK?"

"OK," said the girl.

No one asked whether it was OK by *me*.

I made the most of the rub-down to do a little investigating:

"That girl, was she in an accident?"

"The one who was at the door? I'm afraid I've no idea. She's not on this ward, that I can tell you. She's probably up on the third floor, I saw her using the lift earlier."

Hardly what you would call progress.

The nurse's name is Myriam. She's a buxom forty-something woman, a live wire, she laughs a lot, talks too loudly in her beautiful southern accent, articulating every syllable and embellishing the endings of words with letters that have no place there. It reminds me of my inbred relatives down south. Since she noticed that I still have a faint hint of an Occitan accent, she took me under her wing, and tells me endless stories about every detail her life—probably to keep me distracted. I express my gratitude for this attentiveness by lavishing her with flattering, improbable names: bronzed beauty, young goddess, light of my eyes, spice of my life.

She chuckles, on account of my age. If I were fifteen years younger she would be purring with pleasure. I've arrived at that baleful age where I make women laugh without even trying.

"And how are you today, my Mediterranean Venus?"

This is enough to get her going:

"People these days, they're unbelievable! Half an hour ago, this guy just roars past as I'm driving out of the emergency department, straight past the stop sign. I leant on my horn, obviously. I mean what would you do?"

It all depends.

At twenty, I would have jumped out of my car and punched him in the face.

At thirty, I would have given him the finger and hoped he was spoiling for a fight.

These days, my courage is inversely proportional to the size of the other guy.

It's amazing the way that age can make a man more forbearing.

That said, Myriam's question was clearly rhetorical, because she rambles on:

"… and he screams at me 'Silly Bitch!' Those were his very words. Scuse my language, but honestly! I was just itching to take a swing at him, I can tell you…"

She is still angry, I can tell by the way she is scrubbing my bits with the rough flannel. So as not to fuel her anger and risk a fatal accident, I express my sympathy with little anxious nods, holding my breath, staring straight ahead, pupils dilated. Eventually she calms down and I can breathe again.

While she's about her business she informs me, in her thick Bordeaux drawl, that they'll soon remove the drip-*uh* and the drain-*uh* and raise me to a semi-sitting position.

"That way, you'll soon be able to wash your own bits."

I stifle a sigh of relief. I know there are people who fantasize about getting a bed-bath, but the reality is deeply disappointing. Myriam has all the delicacy of a stretcher-bearer on the front lines in the middle of a bombing raid, she has a younger colleague who is painfully ham-fisted and an older one whose hand hovers over the area for so long that the water has time to evaporate before it hits the spot. I prefer to look after my tackle myself. I take no pleasure in it, but I'm efficient.

As Myriam packs away her kidney tray and her bottles of Betadine, she says:

"Oh, yeah, I forgot! The physio will be visiting you from tomorrow morning to mobilize you."

"To what?"

"Oh, don't worry, you're too old to be going off to war! Mobilize means getting you to be a little more mobile."

"Already?"

"Don't get your hopes up, you've a long way to go before you can take me out dancing!"

She gives me a wink. I laugh long enough to make her happy. She is still giggling as she leaves the room. I call after her to close the door.

But of course she is long gone-*uh*.

M AYBE IT's the prospect of my looming expiry date that makes me want to rake over the past. I'm just saying, I mean, what would I know, I've no experience.

This is my first time being old.

Whatever it is, I'm hardly four pages into my autobiography and already I'm struggling like a nun in a brothel. It's not easy, let me tell you. Not easy at all.

There are whole swathes of my life I've forgotten. There are other bits where I can't be sure to within four or five years when they happened. And then there are memories that are crystal-clear. I've discovered—it was high time— that the preciseness of a memory has nothing to do with the importance we attach to that memory.

For example: I can remember the taste of the worming powder my mother used to give me, the smell of the wax polish she used on the furniture, and of the purple ink and the white paste we used at primary school. But I don't remember the smell or the taste of my first love. Any more than I remember the others, and there aren't a whole heap.

And yet, in the hierarchy of vivid memories, my first conquest should surely come a little higher than the tubes of Etuifont powdered ink we had to dilute in a huge water barrel or the little pots of Cléopâtre paper paste made from starch and bitter almonds.

I can tell you the precise colour of my first bicycle, a red Peugeot with back-pedal brake, a bit too big for me, with mudguards, rack, headlamp and chain guard in the same colour and beige panniers.

My father's eyes, on the other hand, I'm not sure: blue-green, grey-green, grey-blue?

I can remember every last flagstone of the barracks where I spent sixteen months doing National Service, but I would be incapable of sketching from memory the buildings of the secondary school where I spent eight years, from *sixième* to the *baccalauréat*—including having to repeat *troisième*.

I cannot remember a single voice.

Not one.

I might as well admit it right now: I don't have much to show for my sixty-seven years here.

Everything is slipping away, everything is flashing past.

I should probably be happy: if you want to get somewhere far away, it's best to travel light.

Except, I'm not sure I'm going to get very far.

E VER SINCE SERGE and I met up again, yesteryear has started to feel like yesterday.

We quiz each other, what year was this film or that song released? What was the name of that guy, that girl? It forces us to revise, to do our homework, and since we don't have to worry about getting bad marks, it's not disagreeable.

When I'm not writing my life, I spent a lot of time on YouTube—thanks to my great-nephew, who showed me how it works—listening to Eddy Mitchell, Johnny Hallyday, Long Chris et les Daltons, Vince Taylor, Elvis the King, Dany Logan and Paul Anka. I close my eyes and dive into the past. Every song reminds me of a hop, an old flame, a slow dance, a French kiss, *Put your head on my shoulder*, the crushes I had back then, Michèle, Yvette, Anne-Marie, Danielle, the checked shirts and the polka-dot dresses. All those girls who clung to our imaginary washboard abs as they rode on the back of our mopeds—the Solexes, the Mobylettes, the Vespas.

In those blessed days of end-of-dance scuffles, when guys would push and shove each other a couple of times to avoid throwing an actual punch, when the worst injury possible (and the sexiest)—narrowly beating a black eye—was a chipped front tooth.

*

Sometimes, I shed a little tear.

It's memory-related incontinence, a sort of emotional bed-wetting.

P ROMISES ARE made to be kept: the physio came that morning. He drew up an Olympic schedule and, over the past few days, we've started my rehabilitation. I say "we" because I feel he's putting in more effort than I am. I can tell he's motivated. He'll be up and about before me.

That said, he's a decent sort of guy, which is just as well for him, given the insane amount of effort he demands of me. He started out gently, with a simple, duplicitous massage just to lull me into a false sense of security, then he moved on to electrical muscle stimulation. Now, he's forcing me to raise one leg a few centimetres, then the other. *Come on—come on—come on! Hold it—hold it—hold it!* And given the pitiful results of my efforts, I can tell I'm not going to be dancing the French cancan anytime soon. Just managing to sit on the edge of my bed is a whole soap opera. I topple backwards like a wounded Weeble with a leg in plaster and a surgical support brace. Every movement has to be thought through, negotiated, and each comes with its own complications, its discomfort, pain and tightness.

I feel like a feeble old codger, which is probably just a foretaste of a not-too-distant future. I thought I could rely on the man I used to be before the accident. Not much of a sportsman, I'll give you that, but a guy who was in pretty good shape for his age in terms of energy and agility.

Disappointment and disillusion.

My abs are as taut as perished rubber bands, my left leg is nothing more than a bolster encased in cement. My pelvis hurts, my back aches, my arms are feeble, my neck is giving me gyp, and the less said about my morning glory the better—not exactly triumphant—or my general uselessness.

I'm starting to pity myself, it's almost moving.

A CURT KNOCK and straight away the door opens. Shit, never a minute's peace!

For once the door was closed and I didn't even get the pleasure of saying "Come in!" The surgeon is already striding into the room followed by a gaggle of startled interns who have barely flown the nest. I should have realized: it's Thursday, 11.30 a.m. The guy is a Swiss cuckoo clock.

He greets me with a military: "Monsieur Fabre!"

Then he whips back the sheet—*abracadabra!*—and two seconds later he is examining me in front of his students.

"Hope you don't mind," he adds, brooking no possible objection.

I can tell that if I say, "I do mind," he'll likely shatter my leg again.

I resolve myself to kowtow to this mandarin, since there is every reason to think that I will need his services in the days to come.

The consultant itemizes my injuries and the repairs that he has undertaken for the benefit of his students. Only now do I realize just how smashed-up I was.

I have the vague impression that, by his lights, he is doing me an honour in selecting me as the object of today's lecture: *Musculoskeletal injuries in the elderly patient.*

By rights, I should thank him for stripping me naked in front of the three lads with bags under their eyes and the two ashen-faced girls who now stare, embarrassed, from the foot of my bed, from where they have a bird's-eye view of my antiquated plumbing.

I feel about as relaxed as a frog on dissection day.

I'm not particularly prudish, but I prefer to flaunt my athletic physique to a select group of my choosing, one at a time, and all of the fair sex.

On this occasion, I notice that modesty increases with the ravages and flaccidities of age. I feel sure that I would not have felt so self-conscious in the days when I had abs by the six-pack.

Visibly, such considerations do not trouble the specialist, who is prodding me with his calloused fingers, and he continues to recount my case. Technique faultless, respect slapdash, compassion optional. To him, in this precise moment, I am not *someone*, I am an exemplary piece of work with an excellent prognosis for recovery. There is no point grimacing when he presses too hard, he will not notice; he sees only my scars.

If, one day, I manage to walk properly again, I'll owe it all to this expert in scalpel-wielding and human relations. I know that. Even so, I can't help but think he was only doing his job, and he was well paid for it.

Gratitude stems from the compassion people show you, not from their skill. The surgeon has all the warmth of a fridge and inspires about as much affection. But I suspect he does not give a damn, and for that I can hardly blame him.

He finishes his examination and concludes "Perfect!", absent-mindedly tossing the sheet over me, leaving one leg still exposed to the four winds.

Then he stalks out, followed by his flock, who mutter their timid goodbyes.

They leave the door open.

I try vainly to grab at the sheet.

M Y FIRST TIME in custody, I had just turned eight. I had scrawled *Laferté is a viscous bastard!* in red chalk on a toilet wall. Monsieur Laferté, my teacher, informed by some brown-nosed snitch, caught me in the act as I was adding the final exclamation mark.

I remember crossing the vast playground, dragged by my teacher, who gripped my ear painfully between his bony fingers. I was moving faster than my legs would have liked, headed straight for the headmaster's office, without a thought for the games of marbles and hopscotch. Like a republican guard of honour, the pupils silently parted to let me pass and I could see the respect in their eyes. I had *slagged off* my form master, I was fruit for the gallows, I had the makings of a convict, I was a true outlaw, a Mémé Guérini.

There are some moments of glory in life that are incomparable.

My teacher relayed my misdeed to the headmaster, Monsieur Respaud, mopping his damp forehead with a checkered handkerchief. The headmaster eyed me scornfully. Then, rolling his Rs, since he was a native of Foix, he said:

"Are you proud of your actions, boy? Look me in the eyes, sir."

The headmaster addressing one of us as "sir" filled the air with crystals of ice, turned our bowels to jelly and filled our mouths with cotton wool. If I was determined to prove that I had something in my Y-fronts, it was now or never. Might as well confront the Medusa: a single glance and I was turned to stone.

I was treated to a protracted, purgative harangue about respect, consideration, theft of chalk, defacement of walls, appropriate choice of vocabulary, the Republic and spelling.

"Orthography, lad! Or-tho-gra-phy!"

Arms folded, lips pursed, my form teacher greeted each phrase with a solemn nod.

When the bell rang for the end of break he went back to class, leaving me hostage. Monsieur Respaud had me sit at the dunces' desk next to the stove.

"Take you your copybook, sir!"

Whatever my punishment, it would be grossly unfair, all I had done was proclaimed the truth to the whole world: Monsieur Laferté was a cockroach in a grey smock who made our lives a living hell and screamed at us for the slightest thing. Everyone hated him, especially since our previous teacher, Monsieur Petitjean, had been the sort of gentle giant of infinite patience we all wished was our father.

The headmaster must have agreed with my assessment, because in the five hundred lines he made me write, there was nothing about the tenor of the insult, merely the distinction *Viscous defines a liquid as viscid or sticky; vicious qualifies a person as cruel and mean.*

At the time, I remember thinking we were on the same wavelength.

Monsieur Laferté was a bastard, but a *vicious*, not a *viscous* one.

If you say so.

They contacted my father at the factory—we had no telephone back then. He collected me at 3 p.m. on the dot, after the lunch break. Everyone else had gone back to class. I was scrawling out lines spattered with ink blots. Through the window, I saw him push open the gate and stride across the deserted playground. I saw his balding head pass beneath the windows of the headmaster's office. He rapped twice on the glass door and Monsieur Respaud gestured for him to come in. My father greeted him with a booming "Monsieur Respaud!", though he called him Émile at the local Workers' Party meetings. But this was no time to blur boundaries.

He listened to the account of my crime without turning a hair, rigid and upstanding as justice, in his shabby overalls and his cap pulled low over his forehead. In his eyes there was no pride and no respect. On the contrary, a storm was brewing. My glory was crumbling, farewell to the gold stars and the laurels. I had arrived a valiant resistant, admired by my peers, I was leaving in disgrace, a shabby little troublemaker, a feeble rebel with a poor grasp of adjectives.

The headmaster gave a detailed description of my inattentiveness, my incompetence and my insolence. Then, shaking my father's hand, he concluded:

"I regret to inform you that your son is a bad element, Monsieur Fabre."

Eventually, we crossed the deserted playground. In the infant classroom they were singing 'Frère Jacques' out of tune. All the way home my father did not utter a word.

It is a long road that leads to the slaughterhouse.

I remember my mother's panic when I arrived home with my father in the middle of the afternoon. Was I injured? Sick?

Shamelessly adding dishonesty and cowardice to the list of my misdeeds, I wailed:

"I didn't do nothing!"

My father gave me a slap, then, in a tone that brooked no argument, he growled.

"Go to your room. I'll deal with you later."

There were slammed doors, the scraping of chairs, snatches of muttered conversation, the family council was deciding my case. One ear stuck to the wall more firmly than the suction pads my mother put on my chest when I had bronchitis, I tried to catch a word here and there.

Nothing. Nada. Zilch.

My father sounded furious. My mother's voice was wheedling as though she was trying to find excuses for my actions.

Suddenly, from the council chamber, I heard pépé Jean roar:

"That La-a-ferté is a vic-cious bastard!"

I felt a sudden wave of relief. More than that, I felt vindicated. I was not responsible for my behaviour, my genes had simply performed their seditious duty.

Like great-grandfather, like great-grandson.

Now here I am in dry dock, an unexpected pit stop in this solo open regatta—pelvis smashed in two, leg shattered like a mosaic—taking my bearings, checking the hull and the sails, poring over the charts plotting a course to the next port.

It is not a pleasant thought: sixty-something, worn down to the threads, or almost. A widower with no children, no dog. The beginnings of a cataract, a slight problem with my hearing, a prostate like a grapefruit, basic run-of-the-mill stuff. Some savings that are no use, an apartment that's much too big that I've been intending to give a lick of paint for nearly twelve years. But why, for what, for whom?

For the past seven years I've been *retired*. Being in a mischievous mood yesterday, I looked up the definition on the Internet. Among other things, I found:

"*Retire: (vt)* order a military force to retreat following an adverse encounter with the enemy, or to withdraw from a country it can no longer command."

And the synonyms: "Withdraw, draw back, flee, give ground, beat a hasty retreat…"

Perhaps it is the effect of the morphine or the faint beginnings of serenity, but although I can feel myself beating a hasty retreat, it does not seem to bother me in the least.

I'm getting old, that much is undeniable. I've had time to get used to it. I'm quietly tottering towards that fourth age which—unlike the conspicuous consumers and media darlings in the third age—is of no interest to anyone except opticians, dentists and people who sell mattresses that prevent bedsores. Not to mention the florists, those purveyors of deepest sympathies.

And, when the music stops and the ball is over: the undertakers.

H E COMES IN without knocking and barks a "Hello!" like a slap in the face.

I say:

"Hey, Camille! I didn't think I'd see you again, after my little performance last time…"

"…"

"Come on, spit it out. I won't hold it against you."

I can tell he's pissed off.

"Look, this isn't easy."

"Which bit isn't 'easy', kid? Saying what's on your mind, or being on the game?"

"I swear, you're a complete… a complete…"

I sigh:

"… arsehole, yes, I know. I won't argue with you on that score."

A little practice run is always worthwhile.

"What gives you the right to call me kid?"

"Because I'm an old man. You could be my grandson. But you're welcome to call me kid if it makes you feel any better."

"You don't get to say what I can and can't do. And I'd hate to have you for a grandfather."

"If I were your grandfather, you wouldn't be working the streets, I can promise you that."

He gives a bitter laugh.

"You can't stop yourself judging people, can you? You just can't help yourself. I'm completely disgusted… I dragged you out of the river and I feel, I feel…"

"Fucked?"

Shit, I spoke too quickly. Belatedly, I correct myself:

"I'm sorry, that's not what I meant to say."

He shrugs and goes and stands by the window. Unthinkingly, he runs his fingertips over the venetian blinds, the noise is grating.

Finally, in a soft voice, he says:

"I'm not what you think."

He spins around to face me. I can tell he is fumbling for words. Although he must have practised, rehearsed his monologue before showing up. But now he is standing in front of me, the words won't come.

I throw him a line:

"So, why do it? Drugs?"

"No, of course not! I'm clean! I don't touch that stuff."

"Why, then? For some pimp whose only job is to come by to read the meter? Not that it matters to me, you know, but I'm curious. Maybe someone saving my life has made me curious. I'd like to understand."

He gives a sardonic pout.

"You'd like to 'understand'? Oh, it's not difficult. Do you know how much rents are, how much it costs to buy food, to buy books?"

"Because you're an avid reader, I suppose?"

"What's with the hoary old clichés? Why shouldn't I read? Because I'm young? Because I 'turn tricks', as you put it. I'm studying for a degree in maths and physics. I want to work in nuclear medicine. I have an entrance exam in June, and places on the course are very competitive."

I'm gobsmacked. It must be obvious: for two seconds, his eyes blaze with pride.

That shut the old bastard up.

He makes the most of this to tell me about his life.

Life isn't exactly a bed of roses for young Camille, to put it mildly.

No one to help out, no scholarship, no job he can find to fit in around his lectures and his studies, except for minimum wage.

"I live in a cupboard ten metres square with rent so high I practically have to sell a kidney every month. The real pimp here is my landlord. So that's why I… we… you get the picture. I do what I do so I can carry on with my studies, and I hate it. Do you 'understand' now?"

"Don't you have any family?"

"In my family, we don't like queers… I got the hell out two years ago, I'm sure as hell not going begging to them now."

His voice cracks a little. He's had a fucking hard time of it, the little snowflake. He clears his throat and carries on, trying to sound detached:

"Not that it matters, they wouldn't have the money to help me anyway. I get by, I do what I have to like everyone else."

"You mean there are other kids who do that?"

"Are you really that stupid? Do you think going to university is free? That every student gets a room on campus? You really need to get out more."

He is now sitting on the chair, one buttock perched precariously just like last time. Ready to run at the slightest sign. He talks, he talks... he tells me about his fucked-up life. The boyfriend he shared the flat with who unceremoniously dumped him at the start of the academic year; the loneliness, the hardship, being forced to find a studio apartment urgently. But with no money and no one to put up the deposit, you quickly end up in dodgy neighbourhoods and insalubrious rooms.

He is blessed with an unflagging optimism, because he insists that he's "been lucky": he has managed to sub-let a studio from a fellow-student who is on an exchange programme abroad for a few weeks.

"It's not legit, but I don't care. I'm sorted for the next month at least."

A month... and then what? He doesn't want to think about it, cannot even bring himself to formulate the question. He has burnt through all his savings, he looked for jobs to make ends meet, but they all entailed missing lectures and encroached on his revision time. One day, some guy told him that, in order to get by, he was a *casual hustler*...

"Jesus Christ, there's a *name* for it?"

"There are names for everything."

He's right—"casual hustler" makes me think of oxymorons like "surgical strike" and "collateral damage". There really are names for everything.

Even the worst of things.

He stops.

I gesture to him, *go on, go on*, and so he does.

Touting for business online or in bars, the furtive encounters, outdoors weather permitting, otherwise in public toilets so he can avoid bringing punters back to his place. Giving out his address would mean taking a risk. There are a lot of twisted people out there.

"Girls have it easier, they can always work as escorts, sometimes they might even get away without having to have sex. But for us…"

Us… guys.

"Really? Is it different for guys?"

"Well, yeah… there's a lot of casual hooking up on the gay scene. Online, in saunas, in nightclubs. These days, the guys who have to pay to get laid are the ones no one wants to fuck."

He doesn't need to draw a diagram: the degenerates, the losers.

"And you really don't have any other option, no?"

He stretches his legs out, helpless, silent, shoulders hunched, eyes glazed.

"Life's a fucking bitch."

Sometimes I come up with just the right phrase.

Hi! Since I've been here, I've learnt a number of fundamental things: I'm old, students of both sexes are turning tricks to fund their studies, teenagers are insufferable, I hate hospitals and hospital food is disgusting, though there may be a connection between those two. Take it as a spiritual awakening. No need to thank me.

Right, just exactly what meds are you taking? Have you been seeing elephants?

I'm not taking anything, and I've never been more clear-headed in my life.

Oh you poor deluded bastard, you've never been clear-headed in your life. And I've got the photos to prove it... And don't talk shit—you can't possibly be old, you're a year younger than me.

And on that subject, give a little thought to the wise words of Maurice Chevalier: "When you start forgetting to button your flies after you've pissed, it's a bad sign, but it's much worse when you forget to unbutton them beforehand."

Assuming you haven't reached that stage, all is not lost, take my word for it.

Thanks for putting things in perspective. I'll try to keep a sense of proportion. Thank you for putting balm on my wounds.

Speaking of balm, wait until you taste the kouign-amann I'm bringing you, it is an authentic religious experience: heavenly voices, the white light at the end of the tunnel... Once you've eaten it, life will take on a whole new meaning. You will be transfigured.

What do you drink with it?

Excellent question... Dry cider, to be authentic to the region? But I might just as easily suggest a Coteaux-du-Layon, a Vouvray, a little Jurançon, a late-harvest Riesling, champagne, maybe, or sparkling wine?...
   So many paths that lead to happiness.

Maybe you could organize a tasting?

Duly noted. I'm pleased to learn that your case is not entirely hopeless.

Not entirely hopeless, I'll grant, but pretty worrying. I need a lot of care and attention.

I'll make sure to bring all necessary provisions, in keeping with my boundless generosity.

T HIS MORNING, I managed to get out of bed all by myself. The physio doesn't really recommend it, it's a little premature, but I don't give a toss, I can't lie around in bed any longer.

Swept along by a vague sense of elation—and to leave the field clear for the cleaning operatives—I went so far as to try to make my escape down the corridor. Hobbling with my Zimmer frame, I made it as far as the seating-area-cum-waiting-room, a distance of 10.5 metres. I collapsed into an armchair, completely exhausted. To save face and to give the impression to all and sundry that this was where I had been headed, I perused a few of the magazines on the glass coffee table.

Investor's Business Daily, Forbes, Management, Capital.

A selection of magazines carefully chosen to encourage distraught patients to dream of a brighter future, and provide light relief for families, allowing them to check the FTSE and the CAC40 while waiting for a loved one to be wheeled out of surgery.

As I got up to go back to my room, and much against my will, I caught a glimpse of myself in the large mirror behind the fake pot plants. I admired the overall appearance. Especially the stylish hospital gown that falls to mid-thigh and is generously open at the back, allowing the whole world to admire my hirsute buttocks.

But you try putting on a nice suit, or even a pair of Y-fronts at my age, with my pot belly, with one leg in a plaster drainpipe from crotch to ankle.

In my room there is no mirror, except for the one above the washbasin in the bathroom. I feel no real need to look at myself. Me, myself and I are an old married couple. The narcissistic spell is long since broken.

And now, for the first time in months—or years, as likely as not—I came face to face with a vision of myself—in a full-length mirror to boot.

I headed back to my bachelor pad with a solemn soft-slipper shuffle. The room reeked of rubbing alcohol and disinfectant. I went straight into the bathroom. It's roomy—designed to accommodate wheelchairs—and, affixed to the back of the door, there is a good-sized mirror that I have thus far had no need to use.

I slid home the bolt, and, in strict privacy, I slipped off my nightie.

If I had to choose a word to describe myself, I think "subsidence" best fits the bill. My whole body seems to have suffered a landslip.

As far as my face goes, this is hardly news, I shave every morning. My big almond eyes have long since drooped to bloodshot bloodhound. The face has slipped somewhat, the neck jiggles a little, but I still have a high forehead. So high in fact that one of these days it will join the back of my neck. On the other hand, I am astonished to discover that I have reached that glorious age where firm pectorals are transformed into flabby dugs, when the belly hangs over the pubis, where the proud testicles, once comfortably nestled in a scrotum as snug as a pair of bikini briefs, are now pendulous bell-clappers in desperate need of a jockstrap.

Given time, I should be able to do even better: lose a little more hair, mislay a tooth or three.

Decline and fallout.

It was at this point in my inventory of fixtures when I heard the girl's voice.

"I'm just borrowing the laptop, don't worry, I won't be long."

From the bathroom, I yelled "Hey! Hey ho! No-no-no!" I hurriedly made myself decent and threw open the door.

Too late, the little minx was long gone.

I rang for the nurse.

I kicked up the obligatory fuss: shock, indignation, anger, etc.

"*What* girl?"

She seemed exasperated. This was the last straw. I described her as best I could.

"Oh, yes… that vaguely rings a bell. I'll make enquiries."

I didn't need her to make enquiries, I needed her to track

down the bitch with the floppy fringe, exterminate her and bring me her head and my laptop.

The nurse flared her nostrils, making no attempt to disguise the fact that she didn't give a tinker's curse about my misfortune.

"You have to realize, these things happen, even in hospitals we're not immune to theft…"

An audacious admission, and one that helped to move the conversation forward.

"I'm not accusing anyone of *theft*," I said. "That girl took my computer without my permission while I was in the bathroom. She said she was borrowing it."

"Really? Oh, well, in that case…"

I saw a slight reproach glitter in her eye. Visibly, she was thinking, "Well if the girl just borrowed it, where's the problem." And she had a point: where was the problem?

I felt old. Ridiculous. Impotent. So, nothing particularly new.

The girl came back after about two hours. She came in without knocking, set the laptop on the bedside table and said with a big smile:

"Wow, pretty cool."

As she seemed about to leave immediately, I indicated to her in carefully chosen terms that to my mind it was not "cool" at all. That I did not appreciate her behaviour and that making further use of my laptop was out of the question.

She stared at me, looking a little surprised. And a little stupid.

"Huh?"

I modified my register.

"Don't even think about coming into my room, OK? Or touching my laptop."

"But *why*?"

It was a cry from the heart.

"You don't need to understand why. Just give me a wide berth in the corridor and don't set foot in this room again."

She said nothing for two or three seconds, her face crumpled—from the effort required by thinking, is my guess. Finally, she launched into a tirade of dizzying speed and improbable language, probably modern lingo, since I did not understand everything she said.

Of the torrent of words, I managed to catch one or two: right, fine, whatever, OK, yeah! And a variety of insults and onomatopoeias. The apparent significance of all this was that I was not cool, no need to do her head in, all right, fine, it's just a computer, fucksake.

The more I looked at her, the uglier she seemed, huge, grotesque, her breasts too big for her height, her hair greasy and dishevelled, a home-made piercing in her lower lip. Not very well centred, unsurprisingly.

And I was being given a telling-off by this little troll.

Suddenly, her voice cracked and she slumped into the chair next to my bed and sat there whimpering, her face in her chubby hands, her bitten nails gracefully painted cobalt-blue.

I picked up my book again and waited for the waterworks to subside. Sobbing girls scare me stiff. I want to turn off the sound. And this particular girl was in a class of her own when it came to noise pollution. She bawled like a baby deer, sniffing and snuffling like she badly needed a handkerchief. Her shoulders heaved like a labourer holding a pneumatic drill.

Just then, a couple wandered down the corridor and, from the sympathetic smile they flashed us, I could tell there was a misunderstanding: a little girl in tears next to the bedside of an old man in plaster, it must have looked like something straight out of a novel by Zola.

Granddad was dying.

The book in my hands was probably the Bible, or an anthology of edifying aphorisms.

I set down my copy of Boris Vian.

I said:

"Are you nearly finished caterwauling, or are you planning to keep it up all day?"

As sympathy goes, I couldn't come up with anything better.

She rubbed her eyes with the palms of her hands like a four-year-old. Girls, I tell you, they're a nightmare.

I attempted a diversionary tactic.

"What do you need to do on my laptop that's so important? Why don't you go for a walk in the park?"

"I'm not allowed to walk. The doctor said so."

Not allowed to walk? Given all that excess weight, I'd have thought it would have done her a lot of good. Modern medicine is a mystery.

"If you're not allowed to walk," I said spitefully, "how come I see you going past my room ten times a day?"

"Cos I get bored. This place really hacks me off."

On this point, at least, we were in agreement.

I almost asked her how long she was in for, but stopped myself just in time. In the first place, I didn't give a damn, and in the second, I don't know the first thing about kids— given my history—but I'm guessing it's much the same as kittens and puppies: if you're dumb enough to scratch their heads it won't be long before they start pissing on the table legs and hogging the sofa. I'll have none of that here, I need my peace and quiet.

A LITTLE student nurse, pretty as a picture, trails after the urologist. He's a feisty forty-something, terribly hail-fellow-well-met, but always in a hurry.

He comes to check the equipment and informs me that today they are removing the catheter. And that it is *mademoiselle* who will perform the procedure. He has her explain the process. She answers intelligently, there is a little quaver in her voice, but she does not falter.

Clearly, she knows what she has to do.

The urologist nods, then gestures to me and says:

"All right then, have at it…"

I'm not sure whether he's talking about me or the procedure she's supposed to perform.

Mademoiselle swallows hard and reluctantly steps forwards, contemplates my todger with an apprehension I can completely understand. The urologist heaves a sigh, *Come on, come on*, tapping his foot.

I'd just as soon he didn't rush her.

"Now, you must tell me if it hurts," she says in a timid whisper.

"Come along, mademoiselle, get on with it!" the urologist chivvies.

With a heavy heart, she grabs my wizened *phallus delicti*

with one tremulous hand and the catheter tube with the other.

I say:

"So, do you take the tube every day?"

The urologist raises an eyebrow, the girl blushes and stifles a giggle. I'm not exactly proud of the joke, but it's therapeutic. I need to make the situation seem less alarming.

She starts over, and as she begins to extubate, she warns me:

"It's probably better if you don't look…"

"Don't worry, I'm a couch potato, I'm always watching the tube."

She gives a little laugh, denting the family jewels in the process, but at least it's all over.

She gives me a quick wipe-down, smiles and says thank you in a tiny voice.

I can't exactly say that it was a pleasure—my joystick is throbbing viciously.

But I'm a big brave boy and I smile.

She leaves first and the urologist gives me a wink.

"You've got the knack. Personally, I've never been able to make any of the nurses laugh!"

As he leaves, he turns back.

"Would you like me to close the door?"

He must be new here.

THE UROLOGIST was wrong, I don't have a knack with girls. I never did. For the longest time I didn't even notice their presence, I rubbed along without even seeing them.

They started to seem more important towards the end of primary school. Obviously, like all my schoolmates, I hated girls. Their favourite pastime was pressing up against the railing separating the girls' school from the boys' and staring at us all through break, nudging each other and sniggering. Thankfully, classes were not mixed, so the rest of the time it was just us boys, in a privileged world of male apartheid with NO GIRLS ALLOWED. Private property, trespassers must have a penis.

Girls were rubbish…

Chattering, giggly, fickle creatures. Hysterics. Fibbers.

I was never getting married, that much was settled.

A year later, in mid-July, I fell stone-cold dead in love with a certain Marie-Annick with a faceful of freckles and hair as red as the fires of hell. She was a year older than me, she was from Liège. Her parents had rented our neighbours' house for the summer. Her mother gorged me with home-made waffles I could polish off in three bites, pig that I was. Her father called me "son", clapped me on the back and, with a theatrical wink, warned "not to go *goosing* his daughter or he would have a bone to pick with me".

I didn't have the faintest idea what he was talking about.

I remember that I had just discovered a technique I still use when in foreign countries: if you don't understand the language, trust inflection, body language and tone. The threats were issued in a good-natured tone. The waffles were heaped with sugar.

This tribe was not hostile.

Marie-Annick and I experienced genuine physical passion: we held hands, fingers entwined. I groped the place where her breasts would be once she hit puberty, she pulled down her knicker elastic and showed me the top of her pussy.

I saved myself for when I had hairs.

We even had two epic French kisses, but since she was afraid of getting pregnant, after that we just pressed our lips together, twisting our faces this way and that while we hugged each other hard.

Movie kisses.

And the rest of the time, we were down at the bottom of her garden playing at having tea parties with her Barbie dolls, far from prying eyes, because I would have died of shame if my friends had seen me sink so low.

Unfortunately, at the end of the holidays she went back to Belgium. I was mad with heartache for about two weeks, then rugby season started and life went back to normal.

No more waffles, no more heartbreak.

After that, there was a long period of calm, followed by a few infatuations that never quite amounted to anything.

Finally, at the age of seventeen, I met Chantal. She was fifteen-and-a-half, with long brown hair, huge grey-green eyes, a pronounced lisp and thighs like a grasshopper. She was my first love. My first experience of the kind of true love that means you are prepared to do anything—steal a moped, enlist in the army, jump off the roof, even pass your exams—to impress your little princess. My father did not exactly approve, far from it: Monsieur Gaubert, Chantal's father, was a staunch conservative who voted for the CNIP. He was not of the same *perspective*; though when it came to perspectives, my father felt that the CNIP were standing over a gaping abyss.

But given that I was the oldest son, and that I was of age to *be courting*, he tolerated my antics. I had the makings of a pack leader. A future alpha male. It was the responsibility of girls to beware of the big bad wolf, and of parents to guard their daughters.

The golden rule, back in those days, was "Lock up your daughters, our son's on the prowl."

Chantal's mother loathed me and made no secret of the fact. The son of working-class socialists, an atheist and a teddy boy! I was the realization of her worst nightmares. An antichrist on a moped who hung out in bars and played pinball during Mass. Whenever she saw us talking out on the square, she would throw up the shutters and bellow: "*Chantaaaal!*" in a voice like a foghorn, as though her daughter were a ship in distress and I a rocky coastline. We met in secret, which kindled the flames of passion better than a can of kerosene. The more we were forbidden, the more we wanted it. How many couples have been brought together by the lure of the forbidden and the pleasure of bugging one's parents?

Every night, Chantal would watch from her bedroom window while I stood and kicked my heels outside the boulangerie. We had devised a system we thought was original: after her parents went to bed, she would open and close the curtains twice, this was our signal. I would go and wait for her on the street behind her house, she would silently creep downstairs, slip out into the garden and wait for me in the shadow of a mulberry tree. I would hop over the wall to join her.

Little Montague and young Capulet would feverishly map the topography of each other's bodies and snog until they were gasping for breath. We did *everything*, except the most important thing, which she was saving for when she got married. Unfortunately, she was well brought up.

I panted and I pawed to no avail and ruined every pair of jeans I owned. She would leave me, her eyes shining with promises, her cheeks flushed, her skirt rumpled.

For two years we loved each other without ever sealing the deal.

Then I met Marie-Jeanne, a curvaceous blonde girl who was a little less principled and a lot more uninhibited.

MYRIAM CLEARLY finds me friendly and amenable. She is forever telling me: "If they were all like you, our jobs would be a lot easier."

"But I never stop moaning!"

"Not at all! If you knew the drama we have to put up with from most patients…"

I can well imagine her job is pretty grim most of the time. But I tell her that the patients have a lot of drama to put up with too. And not just light comedy. They've got front-row seats with unobstructed views to tragedies of pain, suffering, boredom, loneliness and every other kind of unpleasantness.

And they're not paid to be here, and they didn't volunteer.

You can choose to be nurses, no one chooses to have cancer or be in an accident.

She nods philosophically:

"Yeah, you're right, I know you're right! Let me tell you something: if I was sick, I wouldn't want to be in hospital. But, well, when you've got no choice… Anyway, I'll leave you to it, I've got my rounds to finish. Oh, I meant to mention, the consultant won't be coming round until late afternoon today."

She never says "Doctor Smith" or "Mister Jones", it's always "the consultant", as though he doesn't have a name.

She says "the consultant" the way she might say God Almighty.

B EFORE I KNEW where I was, I was sixteen.

I grew up a lot during the summer of '61. Within three months I'd sprouted into a lanky beanpole—scrawny arms and skinny legs with all the grace of a gibbon and about half the IQ.

Pépé Jean observed my growth with the intense fascination of a scientist with a laboratory full of rats. He was constantly prophesying that soon I'd be head and shoulders over my parents. His diagnosis was correct: by November I stood eye-to-eye with my mother.

The following March, I was towering over my father.

Seeing his gleaming skull from above was a lot more unsettling than what Gagarin felt looking down from Vostok 1. My father's balding pate was my space flight.

I looked for any opportunity to stand next to him to confirm my recent rise in altitude. In a family of short-arsed, bullet-headed southerners, 5'8" was little short of a heroic achievement.

On every family outing, the neighbours would turn into a Greek chorus: "My *God!* Would you look at the height of him! My *God*, what a handsome lad he is!"

I was finally a man, give or take a few minor details. Including the instruction manual.

*

When I first broached the dangerous waters of adolescence, my father had begun to worry about my "frequentations". In his eyes, my friends were a bunch of grade-A wankers, a bunch of no-hopers. I didn't give a toss what he thought, and that infuriated him. There was a gang of us, Serge, Lulu, Dany, Patrice and me. All lost now to the humdrum routine of life, all except for Serge, whom I tracked down a couple of months back. We were obsessed with black leather jackets, slicked-back hair, gold-plated rings. I wore my hair like Elvis Presley. I was fanatical about weight-lifting, spending hours pumping iron so I could have bulging biceps and abs like concrete.

For two or three years my conversations with my father were reduced to long, sullen silences punctuated by arguments. By day I was petulant and moody; at night I would sneak out. If, by chance, he noticed, he would wait for me to stumble home, sitting at the kitchen table, doing his crossword, chewing the end of his pencil, while the pendulum on the clock ticked like a metronome. When I finally arrived, my breath fragrant as an oil tanker, he would bawl me out in hushed tone so as not to wake my mother. He blustered, he threatened, he raised his fist, but never carried through.

I pretended I wasn't scared of him.

I was broad-shouldered now, my voice had finally dropped an octave, no one was going to curb my hormones or bust my balls. I wasn't some snot-nosed kid any more, I was a man.

Pépé Jean, who got up at dawn, was a privileged witness to our matutinal slanging matches. He acted as referee, keeping score between my father and me—I was always trailing by several points. He took pleasure in tipping oil on the flames by the drumful, chiding my father for being weak and predicting a lifetime of troubles for me.

I wanted to say that the greatest millstone round my neck was him. But I never found the words to tell him.

During calmer periods, my father would badger me about my future.

He wanted me to follow him in the glorious world of French railways. He had boundless ambitions for me: I would be promoted, pass competitive exams, rise from humble train driver to conductor. Maybe even station master, who knows?

This man who had wasted his life fighting futile social battles wanted me to be on the other side, on the side of the graduates, of bosses—little or big. To "go up in the world", this was all he could say. His working-class dream was for me to be a middle manager. He sang the praises of life on the railways, the career prospects, the job security. And the more he talked, the more bored I was already.

Me, I dreamt of adventure, of Russian roulette in seedy dives, loose women, clandestine brothels.

I wanted a life less ordinary.

I N HERE, you don't *have* a fracture or an illness, you *are* the fracture or the illness.

I'm "pelvic fracture, Room 28".

I don't even want to imagine the daily humiliation if I were hospitalized with swollen testicles or a bout of haemorrhoids.

I COME ACROSS an article on male prostitution in Morocco. And I think of Camille.

I behaved appallingly.

I talked to him with the condescension of those who think themselves wise because they're happy to say what they really think. As if being sincere were the only qualification you need to have an opinion. "If I had a kid, it would kill me to know he was doing what you're doing."

How could I have the gall to say something like that to him?!

Always got to stick my oar in. Me and my big mouth—and my pompous fuckwittery.

He's had it tough, the kid, he's been through the wringer. I remember the crack in his voice when he said "In my family, we don't like queers…"

I'm guessing his parents were ashamed of him and booted him out, the way a disappointed customer might send back a product.

We'll have none of that sort of behaviour in this house, thank you very much.

In the kingdom of the blind, the one-track mind is king.

They should see him now, how brave he is. It takes a lot of guts to put up with the shit he puts up with and still have the will and the determination to succeed.

If he lived in Thailand or in some Brazilian favela, people would think he was brave, they'd make documentaries that would bring the audience to tears. Over there, he'd be seen as some kind of hero.

Here, he's just a rent boy.

Camille is a decent guy, and that's not something you see very often. Not only did he save my life, he went down to the police station to give a statement at the risk of having the cops question what he was doing there that night, or any night, he even took the trouble to come and visit me. And what do I do?...

I'm well placed to criticize arseholes, if there were an Arseholes United F.C. I'd be centre-forward.

"IF YOU'VE COME for the laptop, you can't have it, I've got an email to write."

"Whatever, I don't care, it's not like I've got somewhere to be."

She sits down.

She is staggering in her brazenness, this girl.

"… Wh?… Are you planning to just sit there?"

She shoots me a jaded look, toys with a pimple on her cheek, examines the soles of her slippers, sighs, sits down, curls up and says nothing. She looks like a doughnut in a tracksuit. It has to be said that she spares no effort when it comes to watching her waistline, she's forever nibbling something or other. To make matters worse, she's got an MP3 player round her neck, headphones dangling, blaring out some gloomy bass-heavy beats, *boom! boom! boom! boom!*

I hesitate over the best course of action; do I lash out at the iPod with my crutch or call for help? I nod towards the iPod and say:

"Could you turn off the thingumajig, there? It's doing my head in."

She turns it off without so much as a whimper.

Out of the blue, she attempts her most winning smile and says:

"It's my birthday."

Hallelujah!

The effort has clearly exhausted her and she falls silent again.

I tap out a couple of words to Serge, but it's no use, I can't concentrate any more.

There are some people with whom silence becomes as itchy as eczema.

For one reason or another—good manners or simply sheer exhaustion—I finally ask:

"So, how old are you?"

"Fourteen."

I attempt a cunning manoeuvre:

"Your parents are bound to come visit you on your birthday. They're probably waiting up in your room, don't you think maybe you should go see?…"

"Not much danger of that, yeah?"

Shit. Is she an orphan? Just in case, I say:

"Sorry…"

"Don't be, I don't care. So are you done or what? Cos I really *need* to get…"

"… on Facebook, right?"

She smiles.

"Yeah-but-no, I just want to check out something about names. What they mean, that sort of thing."

I have no idea what she is talking about, and it doesn't matter. I can tell I won't get any peace if I don't give in, and I will give in, that much seems obvious. My imminent capitulation seems inevitable. My willpower has become more rickety than a wardrobe riddled with woodworm.

A few years ago, I would have kicked her into touch faster than you can say Jack Robinson. Orphan or no orphan, what the hell do I care?

No, here I was, about to say yes to this parasite out of what? Compassion? Desperation? Woodworm?

Or worse, I'm getting soft in my old age.

M Y SISTER-IN-LAW came to visit. Marie-Christine, Annie's sister. Probably given a heads-up by my brother, not that I asked him.

We exchange a few pleasantries, helped along by current events: a glorious hurricane, hundreds of casualties, houses ravaged, terrible news for insurance companies.

Just as she is about to leave, Marie-Christine tells me to stay strong and accept this ordeal as a test sent by God. I tell her I'm a little sceptical as to the identity of the sender. She sighs mournfully.

She is a God-fearing woman, not that that bothers me, as long as she keeps it to herself. But she has to drag God into the equation at every possible opportunity, as though He were the sole possible answer to any and all questions. In her case, He is: she is a believer. I'm not.

Hence the schism.

She and I do not share the same world view. We mix about as well as oil and water. Beat us all you like, we will never form an emulsion.

Maybe it's a family thing.

Pépé Jean reacted to baptism the way others react to vaccinations and became a virulent atheist. My father was atheist too, but without the proselytizing. He saved his harangues for strikes and the managerial classes. Each to his own evangelism.

My mother? She avoided all subjects that might be "contentious": politics, money, religion. We had no need of them, between pépé, my father and me, we had all the material we needed when it came to squabbles and slanging matches.

Me, I'm a non-believer and proud of it. If people believe, if they don't believe, that's their business. Everyone has to find their own way deal with life, with death, with unanswerable questions and unavoidable doubts. But don't come round interfering and telling me what I should believe or how I should act.

Marie-Christine is devastated, she believes it is her duty to open my eyes. I am her noble savage just waiting to be saved. She is a good Christian. She is an almighty pain in the arse.

I have no time for missionaries, with the obvious exception of the position.

Marie-Christine, like all dogmatists, cannot understand my heresy. I tell her that religion tends to bring out the worst as well as the best in mankind, a theory that is easily demonstrable, from the glory of cathedrals to the atrocities of the Crusades and the Inquisition.

It is not belief that bothers me, it is what believers do with it. People have killed and will go on killing in the name of some hypothetical God, to whom—should He exist—they attribute a plethora of mediocre human qualities. When it comes down to it, I'm not sure whom I fear more, the brutal fundamentalist or the oleaginous proselyte. Each proclaims *his* God, *his* precepts, *his* sacred texts to the world, like banners in a football stadium. Fanatics are just a bunch of hooligans: dangerous, aggressive and obsessive.

"I'll say a prayer for you," Marie-Christine tells me.

God be praised.

I'D ALMOST FORGOTTEN that my room is equipped with two beds.

I have a companion in suffering. They brought him up from surgery a little while ago. He is bristling with pipes and tubes, he has an oxygen mask, his breathing is heavy, laboured and raucous. I was in much the same state not long ago.

His hair is white, his bony hands are criss-crossed with thick blue veins, he looks very old.

Two strapping orderlies slide him from the trolley onto the bed, "You got a good grip, yeah? OK, on three: one, two…"

I'm half expecting them to toss him the way stevedores toss a sack of cement onto a quay. But, no, the transfer is effected gently.

One of them plumps the pillows, tucks in the sheets. The other flashes grins and says:

"This way you're not on your own! It'll be good for you to have some company."

I give him a queasy smile and bite my tongue to stop myself saying that, personally, I hadn't actually asked.

No sooner is the new patient installed in the room than the whole snivelling family shows up. My relative peace takes a hell of a blow. There are dozens of them, they take up lots of space, the room suddenly seems minuscule. There is an elderly woman—the wife I assume—who has to be helped into the chair next to the bed where she sobs in silence. Her pallor is grey, her eyes red. She is accompanied by three strapping guys and a woman in her forties.

They have shrill, irritating voices, the woman especially, and they talk nineteen to the dozen.

Eventually, the woman comes and takes my chair.

"May I? You don't mind, do you?"

The question is rhetorical, she has already plonked her arse on my chair, flattening my permission.

Two more visitors arrive, a boy and a girl of about twenty who hold hands and stand in the doorway for a moment, disconcerted, devastated.

Then the young girl gives me a vaguely exasperated look, as though I were bothering her. In this family tragedy, I am the interloper.

I can't help it, I was here first.

Myriam comes in—God bless her!—and immediately bellows:

"Oh my *Lord!* It's like a train station in here! Let the man get some rest after his operation! One or two at a time, can't have more than that. C'mon, now, off with you…"

Myriam has a gentle knack of getting rid of people. The room empties like a lanced boil, the walls recede, oxygen rushes back.

The old lady stays behind with one of her sons, the quietest of the three. He looks at me, gives an apologetic shrug and whispers:

"Excuse us bothering you like this, I'm sure you need your rest too."

Try as I might, my irritation instantly evaporates.

"It's my father," he says. "He had an accident on the stairs, a bad fall… He's eighty-nine, so, well, you get the picture… They just operated on him, but there was no bed available in the recovery room: a car accident this morning, it was on the news, twenty seriously injured. So they're chock-a-block downstairs."

I give him a smile, come up with a couple of appropriate, inane platitudes.

The old woman has stopped crying. She cannot tear her eyes from her husband, she clings to his limp hand like a lifeline. Nothing exists but him.

It's strange, I almost envy her her pain.

Being alone means not having to worry about anyone.

D URING THE NIGHT, the old man's condition dete-
riorates, apparently.

A long whispered conference between the doctor, the
anaesthetist and the duty nurse takes place at his bedside
in the glow of the night lights. I hear him whimper, hear
the rasp of his breathing under the mask.

The cortège goes out into the corridor, I don't even call
after them to close the door.

I am thinking that soon the old woman will have no
hand to hold.

I can't get back to sleep.

Death makes us think of death, by association of ideas I
suppose. Other people's remind us of our own, of those close
to us, of the possibility of our own demise. This "possibility"
is the only thing of which we can be certain, but we treat
it with a certain scepticism, as though there might be some
doubt. We live knowing that we are heading towards death.
We pretend it's not there. But all it takes is a road accident, a
relative passing away, a phone ringing in the dead of night,
a doctor pulling a face as he reads your notes and death, that
sleazy old whore, is standing beside you. She lays a hand on
your shoulder and sends shudders down your spine.

If young Camille hadn't fished me out of the Seine, I wouldn't be here now. I'd be dead, simple as that. My heart would have stopped beating, the brain stopped thinking. Everything would have fizzled out like a TV being unplugged. No one much would miss me, given that I have no children and Annie—with complete disregard for the statistics—passed away before me. The only thing I have to leave is my body. And I'd be happy to give *that* away here and now.

But though I'm open to offers from anyone, people aren't exactly lining up.

Pépé jean took his leave of us one night at the age of ninety-three.

Not counting my hamster, it was my first death.

We found him lying stiff as a capital I, arms by his side, eyes closed, as though he wanted to do half the work for us by adopting the correct position.

His sense of duty and order was with him to the end.

I hesitated a lot about going up to his room. I had no desire to see a corpse, thank you very much. In the end, I went up out of cowardice because I didn't dare say no to my father. And it was the right decision, because it eased some of my fear of death: pépé just looked like he was asleep, that was all. I'll admit, he looked a little yellowish, but it had been a while now since his skin had gone the colour of old newspaper.

The man from the undertakers asked my parents what they planned to do with the dearly departed, in terms of coffins, flowers, Mass, and all that.

Pépé was a free-thinker, so we steered clear of the holy water. We cremated him in a private ceremony, family only. Not that we could have done much else given that all his friends had long since gone before him and he had managed to fall out with everyone else in the family as a way of saving himself time and obligations.

After the cremation we headed home with the little fake-marble urn.

My parents wondered whether they should mingle his ashes with those of my grandmother, Gilou, but at the thought of having to move her they had qualms.

Mémé Ginou had spent the past twenty-three years in the garage. Pépé Jean had insisted on keeping her there "so she can watch over me while I'm doing my DIY", he told us. He hadn't done any DIY for more than fifteen years, but we left mémé Gilou to rest in peace on the middle shelf between her old Singer sewing machine and her collection of *Paris Match*.

We gave her some peace. God knows she deserved some.

My father and mother held a meeting in the kitchen, they even asked for my opinion, given that I was the eldest son. I didn't care much one way or the other, to be honest, but I valued my birthright all the more because it drove my brother hopping mad.

Should we bring mémé Gilou into the sitting room?

Or send pépé Jean to join her out in the garage?

The problem was, if we brought them into the sitting room, where would we put them? On the sideboard, on top of the TV?

And, well, the garage was an unholy mess…

So, a columbarium, then?

"No, they wouldn't have liked that," said my father. "They always refused to live in a tower block, so they'd hardly be happy spending all eternity pigeonholed with hundreds of other stiffs."

I suggested scattering the ashes and my mother said she would feel weird, sprinkling my grandparents like dust from a vacuum cleaner.

In the end, my father decided we would put them in the ornamental wishing well and plant a tree in their memory.

He and my mother went to choose a cypress tree; it withered and died within two months.

H ERVÉ AND CLAUDINE came to visit and brought me a few books.

I was spared the presence of my niece Aurélie and of Gaël, her other half. In an attempt to excuse their non-appearance, Hervé muttered:

"Look, thing is… they're sorry that they can't be here. They really wanted to come, but Gaël had a seminar in Nice and Aurélie felt she had to go with him."

If the conference had been in Seine-Saint-Denis, I'm not sure she would have been so devoted.

Hervé went on:

"Léo sends his love, we were chatting last night on MSN."

Their son Léo is still in Haiti. He was hardly likely to come back specially for the occasion.

My brother and sister-in-law don't really talk much about Léo, the hippie of the family. At thirty, he still doesn't have a *career path*, and it worries them. They are still hoping he will find himself a "proper job", because voluntary work doesn't earn a man a living wage.

I've given up explaining to them that Léo doesn't give a toss about money. He enjoys helping out disaster victims, building houses out of straw like the three little pigs and waiting for the wolf to show up. And he's in the same boat as they are. Maybe you have to be a little twisted.

On the other hand they're very proud of their daughter, and even more so of her husband, who is the fulfilment of their wildest dreams. You can't really blame them. I think if I'd had children, I might take pride in their deplorable choices too.

My nephew-in-law Gaël specializes in *team-building*, *team learning* and *corporate awaydays*. Just the mention of them is depressing.

The guy is a living exemplar of his work: impeccably groomed, impeccably dressed, pragmatic, efficient and surprisingly hollow. He lives in a parallel universe in which he believes what he does is important. A virtual, utterly pointless and yet apparently necessary world echoing with terms that seem obscure to the ordinary mortal: pyramidal, transversal and matrix organizational structures, actionable deliverables, deployment targets, real-world interfacing.

I have nothing to say to him.

Thankfully, it's entirely mutual.

As for my niece, ever since she shacked up with the *team-builder* she has managed (without much effort) to give up even the vaguest desire to think for herself. She has transformed herself into "Gaël's wife", and has perfectly adopted his way of thinking and speaking, his view of the world, the politics, the fast cars, the flash watches. She has become perfect and purposeless, sleek and decorative. They make a stylish couple, much loved by their banker and blessed by fate. Their one failure is their son Jérémy, who inherited from pépé Jean a contempt for the class system, from my father a fathomless supply of social convictions, and from me (would you credit it?) a practised ease in not giving a shit what other people think. A judicious combination. I'm very fond of the lad.

Having accepted their apologies, ably managing to feign disappointment, we come to the stumbling block. Now that they are here, we will have to *talk*, something my brother and I are incapable of doing. On such occasions, I have to admit that my sister-in-law is a great help. She always comes up with little nuggets of news and gossip, allowing us to weather the regulation one-hour visit to the bitter end.

She launches into it:

"The Tureaus send their best, they say get well soon."

And we're off! Ever since I got here, the whole world has been telling me "get well soon", by phone, by email, by post, via third parties. Give it time, they'll be coming in by carrier pigeon.

"Get well soon"—what a bloody stupid expression.

It makes me feel like everyone is watching with bated breath for me to spring from my bed and do a victory lap of the hospital room. Maybe a triple somersault, a cartwheel or two, would that make them happy?

But I tell Claudine to thank the Tureaus for me. This allows her to keep motoring with no gear change to tell me that the Tureaus are *such* nice people before she moves on to the Morels, the Gonzálezs, darling Ahmed, Pauline and Jo, neighbours and friends of theirs I haven't seen for twenty years—at least—but she talks about them as though they are my nearest and dearest.

She pauses to catch her breath. My brother jumps in:

"The Brunets' son sends his regards. You remember Romain?"

"Oh, he's *such* a nice boy," says Claudine tenderly.

I nod vaguely.

"Oh, yeah."

Something in the tone of my voice makes it clear that I could not give a flying fuck.

Hervé brusquely looks up and shoots me a stoically reproachful look.

Evidently I'm a complete brute, a thick-skinned old bear.

Everything just glances off my fur without so much as leaving a dent.

I DON'T THINK I'll ever know what I was doing on that bridge at five in the morning.

Maybe it was the shock, the stress, the pain, maybe it was something else entirely, but part of the mental hard drive was thrown out with the bathwater. That much is obvious. Might as well just move on.

I've even given up speculating. Five in the morning is too late to be coming back from a movie, a play, a restaurant, going to visit prostitutes isn't exactly my sort of thing, I don't have a dog I need to take out for a piss and, given the season, it's a little early for a morning stroll.

Nothing to be done. It's a black hole.

Not only have I completely forgotten that night, but I can't remember anything in the two or three days before either, maybe more than that. It's hard to say exactly because I don't have any markers. Since I retired, some days are very much like other days, which in turn…

I've noticed a steady decline in my memories and my calendar of events, these days I have enough windows of opportunity to double-glaze a mansion. But, to quote my friend Hervé, who has a fondness for metaphysical expressions, "Fuck it."

In fact, curiously, I've grown to treasure the sense of mystery.

I like to think that one day I'll surprise myself, that it will all come flooding back and I'll slap my forehead and exclaim: "Oh my God! That's it!" like Lieutenant Columbo five minutes before the end of every episode.

The neurologist seems less optimistic. He assures me that after a serious head injury, most people never manage to recover a memory of the accident.

According to him, the glitch is permanent.

The man's a glass-half-empty guy, you can tell just by looking at him. He's forever sighing, constantly trailing off in the middle of a sentence. I'm always afraid he'll collapse before he gets to the full stop.

Maybe if you spend all day hanging out with crackpots you end up a little cracked yourself. He certainly looks to me like he's sprung a leak.

I WAKE WITH A START from a comatose nap, eyes glued shut, tongue like a dry piece of cardboard.

The little minx is sitting at the table.

She glances over at me, says "Hey!", then goes back to surfing the web.

I mutter "leave the laptop", though it sounds more like *lvvee t'lpptopm* and sink back into the arms of Morphine.

When I resurface, she is still there, but now she's sitting on the chair next to the bed.

She is looking at me.

I can smell her supermarket perfume, it's overwhelming, it jolts me awake.

I grumble:

"What is it that you're waiting for exactly?"

She gives a vague shrug, then asks:

"What's your name?"

Caught completely off guard, I say:

"Jean-Pierre."

She shrugs.

"Sounds pretty lame."

"Thanks."

With consummate tact, she tries to make amends.

"Well no, it's not *lame* lame… It's just, like, an old guy's name, you know?"

"A keen observation. Can I enquire why you posed the question?"

Another silence. Interminable. My blood pressure must be through the roof, my heart is hammering in my head, I feel like I'm about to have a stroke and kick the bucket, this girl is a nightmare, she has a gift for winding me up. Finally, she says:

"Me, I like Brad, or Justin."

She pronounces it "Djustine".

Djustine.

Now there's a surprise.

"Or Britney. For a girl, obviously."

Obviously. Nice of her to clear that up. She probably assumes that anyone over sixty is brain-dead. I'm trying to think of some way to get rid of her when she gets up and says:

"I gotta go back. The doctor is doing rounds and we have to be there from the gecko."

"From the get-go."

"Huh?"

"The phrase is 'from the get-go', not 'from the gecko'…"

She pulls a face.

"No way."

Impudent little madam.

"Way. Take my word for it."

"Nuh-uh, I don't *think* so. There's no such animal as a get-go."

*

Fair enough.
Can't argue with that.

My room has become a talking shop.

This morning, it was the little madam with her expertise in zoology. This afternoon, the young cop. Every couple of days he drops in to chew the fat for five minutes. I almost asked him why exactly he visits me, but in the end I thought better of it. I wouldn't want to set him thinking, because he might change his mind and never come back.

He walks in, comes over and shakes my hand, glances at the book I'm reading, pulls up a chair, sits down. Sometimes he just stands at the end of the bed and leans on the metal bar.

We jest, we philosophize.

We've discovered we have a lot in common: old westerns, English comedies, historical novels, the Middle Ages, good food and good wine.

We talk about life, about *society*, that generic term for animals who gather in groups: ants, hunters, golfers, citizens of a country.

I broach the subject of Camille.

"Have you ever heard of this thing, casual hustling?…"

"Yes, sure. It's a relatively recent phenomenon among students, but it's on the rise. Every year we come across a

couple more. They're easy to spot, but what can you do...
Mostly, we leave them in peace. As long as they behave
themselves and there are no drugs involved..."

"Uh-huh..."

"Anyway, what do you want us to do? Fine them? How
would they pay?"

"But you think it's normal?"

He hesitantly forages in his scrubby beard.

"Uh... prostitution, you mean?"

"No, to have to do things like that just to get an education!"

"Oh, that! If I were to give you a list of all the things I
don't think are normal, Monsieur Favre, we'd be here all
day... But no... of course it's not 'normal' at all."

I'm starting to like this guy.

I tell him that, in my opinion, you can judge a society by
the way it treats the young and the old. And I know what
I'm talking about: I don't have any kids. As for what I can
expect in my old age, I'll be interested to see, but I'm under
no illusions. Kids like Camille are not to blame, they're
the victims in all this. They are alarming signs of a more
deep-rooted illness. Secondary symptoms. The velvet on
the mould that betrays the rot beneath.

Maxime agrees with me, and adds:

"But, at the same time... they could find some other way
to earn money..."

"To earn enough to be independent, without missing
their lectures?"

"Well, some of them obviously manage, don't they? They take regular student jobs, babysitting, working at McDonald's, that kind of thing..."

"Well, actually, according to statistics, students with a regular job are less likely to complete their studies. I'm not showing off my knowledge, I found that out on the Internet last night."

"Oh, I believe you, I believe you... The whole thing is going to hell in a handcart! Some of them live on the streets these days... They're students and they're homeless. So I don't find it surprising that there are students involved in casual prostitution. Are you surprised?"

Not in the least.

Hope for the best, but expect the worst. Because we seem determined to make it happen.

I WAS TALKING about pépé Jean. He could take up a couple of chapters all by himself.

I'm not going to claim I was grief-stricken when he turned up his toes. But it was like there was an emptiness in the house. Specifically the armchair.

An emptiness, and a silence.

To be honest, I missed the old goat's bleating, the carping and criticizing all day long. Making my life hell had become pépé's daily occupation. A reason to open his eyes in the morning. It gave him a purpose. More than that, it was a quest.

Pépé Jean may have prolonged my childhood. And I probably prolonged his life.

Most of the time—except when he was doing his best to wind me up—pépé sat in silence, staring into space, head nodding vaguely.

Out of the blue he would start reciting verse, in a booming, dramatic voice, never faltering over a comma, and punctuating the end of his alexandrines by pounding the armrest with his fist.

*

When as, with his children clothed in hides to keep warm,
Frantic and ashen through the menacing storm,
Cain took to flight from the presence of Jove...

Dah-dah-dah, dah-dah-dah, dah-dah-dah, dah-dah-dah...

We would wait for the eruption to subside; my parents
fatalistic, me resigned. I already knew that once the poem
had been declaimed, he would bombard me with questions
I would be unable to answer. I could never remember the
name of a writer, much less that of a poem. My sense of
culture was a little limited, I thought Stendhal was a painter
and Voltaire was a kind of sofa. But there was no getting out
of it, at the end of the recitation pépé Jean would take a deep
breath and let slip the sixty-four-thousand-dollar question:

"So Pie-ierrot? Who's it by?"

I would hazard a guess.

"... Maurice Carême?"

He would roll his eyes and snicker. I hated his guts.

I could have played the senile old git at his own game, I
could have shut him up by reciting some real poetry: test the
bastard's exhaustive knowledge of Johnny Hallyday songs.

For a long time I thought he hated me. From what my father
told me some years later, I was wrong. Pépé was very fond
of me. He thought I had *character*. But he was one of those
people whose throat would have been scalded by a kind
word or a compliment.

My father tried to put it down to his generation.

"That's how things were back in his day. People were reserved. They didn't go around hugging and kissing each other."

Yeah, right.

Pépé was a cantankerous old bastard, a moaner. I must have inherited the gene.

I'm like him; I suffer from constipation of the heart.

TEN O'CLOCK in the morning, and the little bitch is back.

She is a constant scourge: every day she shows up at my door at some point and waddles like a plump little duckling over to my chair.

There she slumps—because she doesn't sit, she slumps—she chews away at her bubble gum, her mouth wide open, so I'm treated to surround sound and Technicolor vision.

I do my level best to be cold and distant with her, and I don't like to boast, but when it comes to things like that my level best is nothing short of stupendous.

It doesn't even register with the Plague of Egypt.

Worse, I think she's actually starting to like me.

More often than not, she simply waits, hulking, placid, for me to give her the laptop. It is impossible to ignore her, to pretend she is not there.

When Myriam passes in the corridor she gives us a little wave.

Last night she said, "She's funny, that girl, the way she comes down to keep you company. It's like she's stuck on you."

*

"Stuck on you" makes me think of rice stuck to the bottom of a pan. Thick, glutinous, difficult to scrape off.

Oh yes, there's no doubt she's stuck on me.

I DON'T KNOW what it's like for other authors. Me, I'm new to this writing lark so I find it takes a lot of time, and forces you to think.

Is it the fact that I'm stuck in this dreary room, where every second counts twice over, and feels twice as futile, that has made me realize only now the scale of the con?

The sheer waste of time, that's what pains me most. Not just the time I'm wasting being here, but all the time I've wasted since I was born. Not the hours blissfully spent doing fuck all, face pressed into a pillow or between the breasts of some girlfriend, no, the whole days wasted.

In life, time wasted is like dark matter, an omnipresent *nothing*, a vast nothingness that occupies all space, or almost. When my story is compacted and all the air sucked out, my sixty-seven years would fit in a Kleenex.

It is the principle of expansion, the soil dug out of a trench takes up more space on the side of the road than it did in the trench, just like the leaves of an artichoke take up more space on a plate after you've eaten it.

At twenty, at thirty, I thought I had all the time in the world, a reserve as vast and inexhaustible as the treasures of an African potentate or a corrupt tyrant.

Now I find myself with a piggy bank that's all but empty. An ugly, shabby porcelain pig rattling with three small inedible chocolate coins.

If I were suddenly to get back all the time I squandered waiting for time to pass, if I were repaid all the aimless minutes, how much I would have in the bank? Months? Years?

Decades, probably, allowing for interest rates.

Life is a shameless con-job: if you're not careful, it will fleece you rotten and send you packing with nothing in your pockets, like a big-time gambler stumbling bankrupt out of a casino.

ANNIE WAS THE ONE who paid for my professional choices, something I only realized when it was too late.

I chose to work abroad. It was a personal choice, but I managed to convince myself that it would be better for both of us: I would earn more money, we would be better able to enjoy life.

Enjoy life? But when?

She quickly gave up on the idea of travelling with me.

The poetry of cargo ports was lost on her, I think. The seagulls' droppings, the cockroaches on the quayside, the foghorns and the smell of sleet were not enough to spark her dreams. Women are difficult.

I wanted to work abroad because it had its advantages, but mostly because, in a foreign country, I felt I was *somewhere else*. Coming from a line of fiercely sedentary men clinging to their roots and welded to their railways, I was the first to cross frontiers, to set foot in countries that I had spent hours daydreaming about, gazing at the huge Vidal de La Blache maps pinned on the walls of my classroom.

In the early days, I think that Annie found it hard being away from me so much of the time. Later, she got used to my absence. And in time, solitude was more bearable than the time I spent at home. You like to think you're independent, you end up becoming superfluous.

In the early days, when I came home, she would ask if I had behaved myself, with the worried yet confident smile of a lover.

One day, she stopped asking the question. Not that I cheated on her very often, though "not very often" is still far too much. Twice in our marriage I had a bit on the side, including once when I was drunk, and can only remember that she was a bottle-blonde.

Two slip-ups in thirty years is a terrible tally. It's too pathetic to be classed as a Casanova, but too high for me to be one of the good guys.

The first girl, the blonde, was one night after a business dinner. The weather was hot, she was hot, the band were pretty good, I'd had a little too much to drink, I'd been away from my wife for three months, the reptilian brain was in control of the beast... I woke up next morning with a hangover and my hand on a breast too big for me to cup.

The second time came much later, she was a Chinese girl, her name was Jiao, which means "beautiful", and it suited her. We slept with each other on and off for three or four years, two fixed contracts, three ports of call.

I didn't exactly show great courage.

Deep down, I'm a one-woman man. Not just because I'm faithful by nature. Part of it is selfish. I find that lovemaking is better when people know each other well. Besides, I don't like hassle.

I'm no saint, I sowed my share of wild oats when I was young. And there were some late plantings too. But it's the aggravation that comes from furtive fumblings that puts me off. Lies and pox and illegitimate kids wheel around clandestine affaires like vultures over an open grave.

Given my line of work, a lot of the guys couldn't understand why I wasn't a skirt-chaser when I was overseas. It's true that in some parts of the world it's easy pickings. I've seen a lot of guys hook up with girls who are barely over-age—to avoid problems. And if they're not quite the right age, most of the time a few notes or a carton of cigarettes is enough for them to forget all about it. If not, they kick up a fuss, claim the girl lied about her age, stumble out of the police station with their honour intact and their wallet emptied, and laugh about it as they get in the drinks because, after all, what can you do, that's just how it is.

You don't get to choose what gets you hard…

I'd like to have a debauched retirement, I'd have my pick of destinations. For twenty euros a month, I could have fresh meat to warm my bed with cooking and cleaning thrown in for free. One of those poor little working girls with dark eyes and bare bellies traipsing barefoot through the puddles and touting for clients outside the bars. And there is no shortage of clients, no fear that sleazy bastards are in decline, they flock to places of abject poverty. Always respectable, always drunk, bags under their eyes, red as lobsters. They disgust me. They're old, they're ugly. They're like me: decrepit, past their use-by date. But that doesn't stop them rubbing their fat paunches, their limp dicks, their sweaty skin up against girls young enough to be their granddaughters.

I know their dirty jokes and their sleazy justifications. "It's different here, it's part of the culture, what do you expect, they need the money, actually you're helping them to survive."

Sad fuckers practically have themselves convinced they're philanthropists.

A FTER ANNIE'S DEATH, I met Clotilde, and a bit later Béatrice.

Clotilde was soft-hearted. She liked to mother me and I was happy to let her, but that's not the basis for a real relationship. We quickly got bored.

If Béatrice had a heart it was anything but soft. No small-talk, no foreplay, no pointless billing and cooing. Nothing but sex and jogging. Sex every morning, jogging every Sunday.

As soon as I'd done the business, she'd leap out of bed and rush to the kitchen to make coffee. She made good coffee.

She dumped me three years ago without a word of explanation to go shack up with a retired PE teacher. I never saw it coming.

Since then, I've been on my own, I've pretty much given up hope, but I'm making great strides towards achieving inner peace.

I drink a lot less coffee.

THE PHYSIO thinks I'm in "great shape". According to him, I'm recovering "remarkably quickly for a man of my age". I suspect he says the same to every other patient on this floor. I'm guessing it's something that's drummed into them during training: *fifty-per-cent-of-recovery-is-down-to-the-patient's-morale*.

And they've got a point, morale is important. I would never have believed it could be so difficult to learn to walk again. Giving up using the Zimmer frame scares me a damn sight more than taking the training wheels of my bicycle. It has to be said that the last time I learnt to walk I was thirteen or fourteen months old, the ground didn't seem so far away, at least I assume it didn't.

It's all a long time ago, I don't really remember.

Four or five days ago, the little madam spotted me taking my daily exercise.

She showed up unannounced, didn't even bother to ask whether she was disturbing me. Why change the habits of a lifetime? It seems to be an acknowledged fact that she is at home everywhere, which is mostly in my room.

I was slowly trudging up and down in front of the window, taking nervous little steps, one hand clinging to

the tripod walking stick, leaning heavily on the physiotherapist.

She watched for a while. Nodded her head and said:

"That's cool."

Buoyed up by this succinct compliment, I would have
given her a thumbs up but that would have meant letting
go of the walking stick, and that seemed a little premature.

I've made a lot of progress since then.

I wouldn't exactly say I'm making great strides, but I
feel as though I am regaining control over this aching body,
which will soon, I hope, be autonomous.

Among the trivial little private pleasures I've rediscovered,
I can now go for a piss all by myself.

I know it doesn't sound like much, but right now these are
the little things by which I measure the fine line that sepa-
rates a normal life from a life in the shitter, no pun intended.

M AXIME COUGHS.
"... Um... I've been meaning to say..."

He stops. It's amazing, this mania people have of going quiet when they've said they have something to tell you.

"I'm all ears, my young friend."

I can tell he's trying to decide how best to tackle the problem.

"Uh... well... OK... the thing is..."

"Yes?"

"You must be wondering why I've been coming to see you..."

"Let's see... My cheerful conversation, my extraordinarily exuberant character, the litheness and grace of my every gesture?..."

He laughs.

"Eh... no."

"No? Well, in that case, I admit, I'm baffled."

He flashes me a half-smile, then—a little more seriously—he stares at me with the eyes of a kid who has been punished for no reason.

"You remind me of my father."

Wow!

I wait for him to continue.

"Actually… you looked so much like him, that first time I saw you."

"When I was in *resus*?" I can't hide my surprise.

"Yes… yes, exactly. Look, I don't really know how to explain it, but the first time I saw you…"

He takes a breath.

"… you looked just like my father the *last* time I saw him."

I can't say I'm exactly flattered, but I'm guessing this is not the moment to open up.

He goes on:

"That's why I came back to see you, at first… because the investigation, well, it's a routine traffic accident, so…"

"So you're saying my case isn't exactly thrilling?"

He dodges the question. He rests his arms on the bedframe, leans towards me and takes the plunge. At least I'll be able to boast that I persuaded a cop to confess.

His father died of a heart attack four years ago in this very hospital. Maxime didn't get the news until late in the day, he was out of the office working on an investigation. By the time he got to the hospital that night, his father was in a coma. He never saw him alive again.

"When I saw you in intensive care, it was a shock, because physically you look a lot like him. And what with the oxygen mask and the tubes…"

I nod. I can imagine the terrible flashback. Now I understand the look he gave me when I first came round. That worried, troubled look of his.

"That's the reason why I kept coming at first. Do you understand?"

"To see *me*, so you didn't have to keep seeing *him*. To exchange your last image of your father for an image of me, an old wreck..."

"Yes, I think that's part of it. Do you find that weird?"

"What I find weird is that you didn't correct me when I called myself an old wreck..."

He bursts out laughing.

If the lad weren't so young, we'd be old friends by now.

I DIDN'T SEE my father die.
I didn't see my mother die.
I wasn't there for Annie.

What is there to add to that?

I'M NOT contemplative by nature. I hate doing nothing. I've always been that way.

I need to move, to do things, to fill up all the little drawers of minutes and hours like a squirrel making provision for the winter.

I traipse back and forth, from the bed to the window, from the window to the door, from the door to the little waiting room, from the waiting room to the nurses' station, where they give a running commentary on my arrival.

"Well, look who it is! Are we taking a little walk?"

"We're making excellent progress!"

"Hello, hello, my little turtledoves…"

Myriam giggles, her colleague laughs too.

I head back, taking baby steps, trying to hold in my stomach, to keep my back straight.

I'm playing the ladykiller. I'm just an old clown doing his party piece.

E VERY DAY, or almost every day, it's the same ritual: I refuse to give her my laptop, she accepts my refusal with remarkable stoicism, then she sits without a word and waits until I've finished using it. Thanks to her, I finally understand the law of inertia.

"Is there no one else who could lend you a computer?"

"Dunno. But you've got yours, so it's all good."

I must have "moron" written across the front of my rapidly balding head.

When I finally give in—and I always give in, it's a nightmare—she seizes the spoils and goes to sit at the little table by the wall opposite the bed.

I have forbidden her from taking it out of the room. She is allowed exactly half an hour, during which I do my best not to fall asleep in case she does a runner with the laptop.

I try to read a little and ignore her presence. It's impossible. She sucks on her chewing gum, whistles under her breath and, for the past few days, she has been sighing every time she moves, like an arthritic old crone.

Obviously, it has occurred to me to do a little investigating, find out who she is, what's wrong with her, but I'm afraid of finding out something horrible, a terminal illness, something eating away at her. Although I wish she were dead every time I set eyes on her, it's only a virtual death, a theoretical demise. I don't *actually* want to kill her. Not yet.

I just want to ignore her.

But the only way to do that would be to get *her* to ignore me.

So as not to have to deal with her unfathomable silences, from time to time I force myself to make conversation. It is a skill at which I've developed a certain expertise thanks to my brother Hervé, a past master at delivering platitudes and silence.

"Did you find out what you wanted about names the other day?"

"Yeah but no I dunno really."

"What were you looking up? Your own name?"

"Nuh-uh, I know my name, so that's sorted."

I laugh in spite of myself.

She furrows her brows, thinks and then corrects herself.

"No, that's not what I meant, I meant, I already looked it up."

"So what is your name?"

"Maëva."

She twists her chewing gum, pierces it with her tongue, and adds:

"It's Tahitian, it means 'welcome'."

"Do you know where Tahiti is?"

She shrugs.

"Yeah, no, I'm not sure… like, Australia I think… Somewhere over there."

She bends over the keyboard, slowly, diligently hunting and pecking with her index fingers, a stray lock of hair across her face. She chews, she snuffles, she sighs.

The girl is the living embodiment of osteoarthritis: a chronic pain to which one gradually becomes accustomed, but which never goes away.

If you could get back something you had when you were twenty that you've lost with age, what would you choose?

I don't understand the question. I haven't lost anything. I'm as innocent and high-spirited as I was when I was eighteen. A vestal virgin.

It's true, the years haven't changed you a bit. That was the first thing I noticed when we met up.
   But seriously?

Seriously? I don't know. I'm thinking. What about you?

I think it would be the urge to "do stuff". I feel like I don't really have any drive any more. I don't get enthusiastic about anything, I don't get carried away, I find everything a drag. It's like there's nothing in life that gets me excited any more, you know what I mean?

Not at all.

OK. Good. So we're in the same boat, then. That's reassuring.
   Even Nathalie is worried, she used to find me annoying, now she just thinks I'm depressing. I think she preferred me the way I used to be.

Well then make an effort, work yourself up into a foul mood! It's not exactly rocket science, for fuck's sake!

I can't get angry any more. I whinge and I gripe and I piss people off, but it's half-hearted, I'm not fooling anyone.

You were never much good at it anyway. Don't take this the wrong way, but you've always been a nice guy, my pathetic friend.

You think it's to do with getting old?

Absolutely not! Take me: insufferable as I ever was. No, it doesn't wear off, quite the opposite, I'd say… Though I have to say you're starting to sounding a bit maudlin. This existential crisis of yours wouldn't just be liver failure, would it?

I have to admit I am feeling pretty washed-out these days. Drinking too much *chouchen*, probably. That said, nothing succeeds like excess…

I THINK I KNOW exactly what Serge means when he talks about his enthusiasm and his urges fading. I can feel them fading too. And I've started to become careful.

Careful, me!

When I was young, I took every risk going. I drank too much, drove too fast, accepted any dare, no matter how stupid or how dangerous. Coming within a hair's breadth of getting killed or getting banged up, that was my whole life.

These days, I'm happy if I can walk twenty metres without falling over. I hang onto my cane, my knees knocking, terrified I'll injure myself. It's shock from the accident, I know that. But thinking back, I realize that I've been too sensible for months now. Handling myself with kid gloves, like I was made of glass. I delude myself into thinking that sixty-seven isn't old age, that I'm still in my prime.

Whereas in fact I'm hurtling downhill on a bobsleigh. Clinging on for dear life.

At twenty, I had more strings to my bow than a politician has offshore accounts: playing rugby, pumping iron, cycling, running, swimming. To pull girls, obviously. Why else would anyone risk pulling a muscle or breaking a bone? No one under the age of forty works out "to keep fit". That's the sort of thing you tell yourself when you're middle-aged and single. Or just middle-aged.

When you're young, you exercise to make yourself stronger, more attractive to others.

To reinforce your position as an alpha male.

Back when I was a teenager, guys ranked each other based on simple, incontestable criteria: having bulging biceps, owning a hot car, being good—or claiming to be good—in the sack, and being able to hold your liquor.

I'm sure it's much the same today, even if the criteria are probably a little different. I'm no expert on the subject of teenagers—far from it—but as a species, they can't have changed that much. Between the age of fifteen and twenty, life is like a wildlife documentary: a struggle to the death for love and for territory. If men pissed in a corner every time they were horny, schools would stink like urinals.

"If youth but knew, if old age but could," now there's a bloody stupid saying…

Health is something we think about only if we've never had it, or if it's failing.

Life is something we cling to only if it's threatened.

Youth is something we can talk about only in the past tense.

"If youth but knew", there would be no gratuitous acts, no hare-brained schemes hatched on distant comets. Everything would be premeditated, meticulously planned, carefully controlled. People would bet only on sure things. So there would be no pleasure in winning. We'd be bored shitless. Better to know nothing, since the prospect of future failures would only discourage us. And having a sneak preview of future happiness would be like opening a Christmas present in November. The present would still exist, but the joy wouldn't be the same.

"If age but could", it would barrel along, never looking back, never getting any wiser, forever ploughing the same furrow, getting bogged down in the same mire. Galloping along at breakneck speed, clinging to the reins. Like an ageing dictator, unable to let go.

It is because we can no longer do certain things that we move on to others. We have no choice. Life drives us down the road, there is no hard shoulder, no junction where we might do a U-turn.

On with the countdown!

But we don't just wake up old one morning, we grow old, we have time enough to prepare ourselves. It's not as though it creeps up on us unawares, so why act surprised?

If I had known, there are two or three pitfalls I might have avoided, certain words I would never have said. Others I would have thought to say more often. Maybe I would have got less worked up about things that didn't matter, I would have made the most of the menu but, broadly speaking, now that I've got as far as dessert—who knows, maybe as far as the coffee—I think that "had I but known", I would have lived the same life.

And "if I but could", aside from ripping off this itchy plaster cast and going home tonight to cook a dinner worthy of the name, I wouldn't change anything. Even hopped up on analgesics on this bloody awful bed in this fucking awful room, I'm happy with the life I've lived.

It suits me, being alive.

I'm not ready to shuffle off my coil just yet, I'm planning to live to be a hundred.

M AXIME STRETCHES, heaves a sigh, massages his neck and shoulders. He yawns like a lion, jaws gaping wide, a clear view of his pink palate.

"Rough day?"

"Rough night, more like it. We staked out a building until four in the morning all for nothing, no result… Then at six, I was called to a domestic… My head's all over the place."

"Your life is an action-packed thriller!"

"Yeah, not so much. In the movies, there's two hours of action and in the end the bad guys get banged up. We spend most of our time pushing paper, taking statements, filing charges, and endless hours doing surveillance in unmarked cars. Not to mention the dealers, the fuckwits who beat their wives, the pickpockets, the guys running protection rackets that we arrest only to release for lack of evidence or who some judge gives a suspended sentence to because the jails are full. It's not Columbo, let me tell you. In the real world, we spend more time dealing with low-level pimps rather than gangsters and serial killers…"

"Maybe, but you like your job, don't you?"

"On days when it goes well and I feel like I'm making a difference, I like it…"

He falls silent, engrossed in his thoughts, or in the haze of lost sleep.

I'd rather change the subject.

Maxime is a truly decent guy, and obviously people hate cops on principle, but when we need them we're relieved that they're there. That said, I'm still wary, for genetic reasons. You don't grow up with a militant left-wing father without feeling a certain caginess when dealing with the police.

I ask him:

"Do you think you could get a message to Camille for me?"

"The kid who pulled you out of the river?"

"The very same."

He thinks.

"… We've got his details in the incident report, it shouldn't be too difficult. What should I tell him?"

"Just tell him I'd like to see him, if he's got a moment free. Try and be diplomatic about it, he's temperamental."

"Really, I found him quite shy…"

I decide not to say any more.

Then Maxime starts telling me about some movie he's planning to go and see, and I don't recognize the title, the director or the main actors, and certainly not the co-stars.

It feels like being slapped with a senior citizen's card.

I have the choice, I can change channels, because I'm culturally ignorant, or I can take an interest. I shrug off my irritation and listen. This guy is a real movie buff. He only ever watches a film in the original language and tries to convert me to the joys of subtitles. I tell him I'm all in favour, except for my eyes, which refuse to read the tiny lettering at the bottom of the screen.

He sympathizes with my infirmity, and I tell him to shut up. Next thing you know, he'll be pushing me into the grave.

F OR THREE or four days I had peace and quiet.

I thought the snot-nosed little madam had gone home. But I celebrated too soon, here she is, on the dot of eleven o'clock, just before lunch, carrying a parcel. Something about her appearance has changed, but I can't put my finger on it.

I put on my glasses.

I see it all at once: the deflated belly that makes her breasts look even more enormous and, swaddled in the yellow blanket, a little sprog, three stray hairs on its head, tiny hands balled into fists, mouth red, eyes screwed shut.

"His name is Justin," she says with a satisfied air.

"Is he… is he yours?" I stammer.

Subtle as always, that's me.

She nods, masticating her greenish chewing gum, then reels off a list of statistics, never pausing for breath, in serious danger of suffocating.

"He was born the day before yesterday at 5.20 p.m. weighing 2.53 kilos and measuring 48 centimetres, he's an Aquarius, I had to have a Caesarean because otherwise there was no way he was coming out."

I nod sagely, unsure whether it is a blessing or a curse to be called *Djustin*, to be an Aquarius, to weigh about five pounds and to be born by Caesarean to a girl of fourteen.

I think it only fair to admit that it never even occurred to me that she was pregnant.

How could I have been so blind?

She doesn't seem surprised.

"I know, I wasn't showing, everyone said so."

I manage to affirm without a blush that her superfluous weight was barely detectable.

"Could you take a photo of us?"

She hands me a digital camera. I can hardly refuse. I take two or three shots of the young mother and her newborn. She holds herself straight, she doesn't smile.

Then she asks if I want to hold her little brat for a minute; horrified, I politely refuse on the pretext that I might drop him.

She pooh-poohs my excuses.

"It's just so I can get a picture of the two of you. You just need to support the head, hang on, there, that's fine."

She deftly places the tadpole into my arms with surprising skill for a girl her age who has been a mother for all of two days. The baby smells faintly of sour milk and vomit.

I stifle the urge to retch.

Once safely cradled in my arms, he opens his eyes, long narrow slits, stares at me as though I were far away, and seems about to laugh.

Stupidly, I announce:

"He's smiling!"

"He's probably pissing. Babies smile when they're peeing, the nurse told me."

Illusions exist only to be lost.

That said, I understand the kid, and this wave of wondrous contentment. Over the past few weeks, I've caught myself smiling happily when I finally manage to empty my bladder.

There are two or three questions I'd like to ask the gymslip mother. Out of sheer intellectual curiosity, no emotions involved.

For example: why the devil has she decided to keep the baby? What exactly is she planning to do with it? She's fourteen, has she any idea of the hell her life is going to be?

But she doesn't seem bothered, not at all. She takes snaps of me and the bonsai from every angle, zoom on, zoom off, with flash, without flash.

The nurse comes in with my lunch and is so startled she nearly drops the tray.

She goes into raptures over the baby, all coochie-coochie-coo, buh-buh-buh, with that sickening facility women have of getting emotional about nothing at all. When she congratulates me on being a grandfather, I am so shocked I'm speechless.

Maëva doesn't even notice, she just says:

"I better go change his nappy, besides it's time for his feed."

And, as she leaves:

"I won't be able to come back until tonight, to go on Facebook…"

*

I only just managed to stop myself saying, "Don't worry, come by whenever you can."

It's not good for me being here, it wears me down.

WHEN SHE HAD her third miscarriage Annie was thirty-nine years old, she had her tubes tied and threw out all the magazines with decorating ideas for nurseries.

We tried to carry on, to make do, and then we tried to *make believe*.

But it's impossible to live surrounded by things unsaid. The questions left unasked and the words unspoken litter the ground like shards of broken glass. After a few years, it is impossible to move without drawing blood.

Everything reminds you of the emptiness: your friends' children, the giggling of kids in the local school; knowing you will never say, my son, my daughter; watching your wife suffer and being helpless.

It contaminates your whole life.

It is like nuclear radiation: nothing is visible, everything is destroyed.

Slowly, we drifted apart, Annie and me, without even realizing. Our mattress developed a hump in the middle, each of us huddled on our side of the bed.

Annie dried up, she shrivelled like a dead leaf. She gave up.

People who have lost all hope are like desecrated
like burgled houses. A warren of ransacked rooms,
lights, shattered doors. Gusts and draughts that n
can stop.

Silence and emptiness.

I was travelling more and more frequently, I lost myself in
my work. My days were busy, active, to me they seemed as
short as shadows at noon.

And Annie was left alone with her solitude.

Unconsciously, I think I chose not to notice her thinness,
the overflowing ashtrays, her uncombed hair, the fluff balls
under the furniture, the bags under her eyes.

Say nothing, see nothing, a comfortable cowardice.

The day she died, I was in Novorossiysk working for a
grain importer.

By the time my parents managed to get in touch, and
I made it to Gelendzhik airport to catch a plane, I got
back too late, much later than young Maxime with his
father.

There was nothing but a slab of marble covered with
fresh flowers and mournful tributes: *To our darling daughter—*
To our dearest daughter-in-law—To my departed sister.

The funeral had taken place the day before. My in-laws
had taken charge of everything.

I had asked them to lay flowers on my behalf, a spray of
blue thistles, her favourite flowers. No ribbon. They could

Earlsfield Library

Issue summary
Patron: 01579****

Item : 90300000714509 , Something to live for
Due:16/06/2022 23:59

Total number of issued items: 1
26/05/2022 09:28

Manage your account online at
capitaldiscovery.co.uk /wandsworth

Call 01527 852 385 for 24 hour
renewal charged at national rates

Thank you for using self service

not bring themselves to do it. Thistles at a funeral, without so much as a note? What would people think?

Instead I was represented by a wreath of red roses garlanded with a ribbon bearing the hackneyed words: *To a dearly beloved wife.* That same phrase—words I would never have written, much less said aloud—was also engraved on the marble plaque surmounted by a pair of stilted doves gracelessly pecking at each other, looking vaguely ridiculous.

I had been cheated of my own goodbyes by that irresistible force, the uncriticizable rectitude of people who mean well.

Sometimes, I would whisper to no one in particular those sweet nothings I had never thought to say to her.

Annie and I had not made love in a long time. So what? We made a curious couple. A cohabitation of two room-mates who dreamt different dreams in a shared bed. But even when hearts no longer beat as one, when a partner dies, a part of us dies with them. When we share our lives with someone, they keep a sliver of it in their pocket. It is their light that is snuffed out, it is we who miss the radiance.

M YRIAM NODS.
        "I can see why you'd be surprised…"

She says this as she buzzes around me like a hard-working bee. Toss the soiled bandage into the bin attached to the trolley, spray freezing Betadine over my calf and my thigh—yow!—clean the sutures with a compress, pick up a clean bandage with a pair of tweezers, deftly unfold it without touching it and lay it over one of the scars.

"It's pretty, though."

"Sorry?"

"Your scars. They're beautiful, neat, clean. No inflammation. All fine."

"Did you notice, though? That she was pregnant?"

"Well, yeah, obviously…"

She says this kindly, but she obviously thinks I'm a senile old fool. Everyone in the hospital probably noticed that the little madam had a bun in the oven.

I persist:

"I mean she's *fourteen*, for God's sake! And it doesn't surprise you?"

"I've got a daughter her age, so no, it doesn't surprise me, it sends shivers down my spine! But, you know, there are worse things. Mostly at that age they come for terminations.

The youngest last year had just turned twelve. I know that because I have a friend who works in Obs & Gynae."

"Twelve?!"

"Yeah. Breaks your heart. The problem is that minors have to have permission from their parents to get a termination. So, between the ones who don't realize they're pregnant, the ones determined to keep the baby, the ones who don't dare tell anyone, and the ones whose parents are opposed to abortion, there are bound to be some who end up like your Maëva. Pregnant, and then…"

"Are there many in her situation?"

"Not as many as you might think, thankfully. We get about a dozen a year on the ward, mostly for terminations, like I said."

"But why don't these girls go on the pill?"

"It's not as easy as that… To go on the pill, you need a prescription. That means seeing a doctor. Talking about *that* to a doctor. Or going to a family planning clinic. Can you imagine how difficult it must be for a girl of twelve or thirteen to go into a chemist and ask for the pill in front of everyone? What if there's a man on the till? What if you live in a village?"

"Maybe, but surely if they're mature enough to have sex…"

Myriam meticulously packs away her bits and pieces—tweezers, compresses, antiseptic.

She looks like a little girl playing at being a nurse.

She shakes her head.

"You really think it's a question of maturity?"

"…"

"Emotionally, intellectually, most of these girls are only twelve or thirteen, even the ones who look like supermodels. They're little girls playing at being grown-ups, or they can't say no to their boyfriends because they're afraid to look stupid."

"Why don't they ask their boyfriends to wear a condom, then? You can buy them over the counter."

"So how do you like making love covered in cling film?"

That was below the belt.

I protest. This is not about me.

She smiles.

"Really? You think so?"

"… well you have to admit it's not really, I mean I'm not exactly…"

"Well, there's your answer then, everyone else is just like you. The difference being that you're an adult, you can accept that there are limitations. Now teenage boys on the other hand… you can talk about AIDS till you're blue in the face, as far as they're concerned it doesn't feel as good wearing a condom. A lot of them refuse to wear them. And if the girl is naïve, or if she's infatuated, she won't insist. And the younger ones are the ones who won't visit the school nurse to ask for the morning-after pill."

As if to console me, she adds:

"But OK, maybe *yours* is a love child. I hope so for her sake. When they get pregnant at that age, it's often the result of rape or incest."

*

This possibility had not even occurred to me, that's how naïve I am. And it's not like I was born yesterday, I know a bit about life and its ineffable pleasures, I've travelled in parts of the world where rape is a sport, where incest is a hobby.

Myriam says:

"Listen, I'll ask my friend if she knows anything more about the girl. Right, I'd better be off, I've still got rounds to do. You're not my only patient, are you?"

That is precisely the problem, I tell her, since it means I am forced to share with others—who don't know their good fortune—the immense pleasure I feel every time I see her.

She chuckles as she leaves. And forgets to close the door.

CAMILLE IS SULKING.

I am making a superhuman effort. No sarcasm, no irony, keep your trap shut Jean-Pierre.

"Thanks for coming."

I can tell he is on the defensive.

"Some inspector told me to come to see you. I didn't exactly have a choice, apparently."

Thank you Maxime, for your unfailing tact.

"Sit down, we need to talk."

Oops! That might have been a little brusque. Camille hardens faster than cooking oil in a fridge.

I carry on, in a more moderate tone:

"I'd like to ask you a favour."

"I've already done you one. I saved your life, remember? But if you want me to do a favour for humankind, I'm happy to chuck you back in the river."

Battleship hit.

I haul myself up using the triangle dangling over my head, I feel a tearing in my thigh and my lower back, I suppress a wince of pain.

"A job, would you be interested?"

"No."

Silence.

I leave the worm to dangle. Camille feigns disinterest, then takes the bait.

"Well… it depends. I've got lectures, like I told you. What kind of job?"

"Not too taxing, not very rewarding, and pretty badly paid…"

He rolls his eyes.

I carry on, unperturbed.

"… but it's flexible hours and comes with free accommodation."

I can tell he's intrigued.

I have thought about this a lot. I will soon be discharged from here and find myself confronted with a daily routine somewhat knocked out of kilter by my convalescence. Physiotherapy, the distance between me and the nearest corner shop, the sheer exhaustion of making it there and back again, the time it will take "at my age and in my condition", as my brother would politely put it, for me to regain the full use of my legs.

"I'd like to suggest you do my shopping, two or three hours' tidying in the apartment a week and, in exchange, in return, I can't pay you much, I don't have a bank manager's pension, but you would have two rooms, a bathroom and toilet all to yourself, rent-free, and use of the kitchen, obviously."

"Why?"

He must have swallowed a puppy this morning. He doesn't talk, he barks.

"I've just told you: to do my shopping, to…"

"No, *why* are you doing this?"

I resist the urge to give him a slap. It might hinder negotiations.

"Because I'm indebted to you, and because it would be useful for me…"

He nervously pushes back the fringe falling into his eyes with the mixture of toughness and grace that informs all his gestures. His pale-blue eyes stare, unblinking, into mine.

He does not say a word.

I answer the question he has not asked:

"I don't expect anything else from you, don't kid yourself, your love for me will have to remain platonic. When it comes to sexuality, I'm very old-fashioned."

He relaxes, almost imperceptibly.

"Listen, it's a serious offer. I'll be discharged from here in about three weeks, I live on my own, things will be tough, and to be honest I'm worried. If you're not interested, it's not a problem, I'll contact an agency and get someone to come in a couple of hours a week, but I thought of you because I know that you're likely to be homeless pretty soon, that's all. If you lived at my place, it would mean I'd have someone there at night, and it would tide you over. And if I have trouble getting my trousers or my socks on in the morning, I'd be less embarrassed dealing with a guy. I just thought that maybe it could be beneficial for both of us."

He tosses his head, flicking his hair back. He hesitates.

"When would I have to let you know?"

"Sometime in the next two weeks. I need to find someone before I move back home."

"I'll think about it."

"You do that."

I open the drawer of the nightstand, take out my keys and proffer them, with a folded piece of paper.

He looks at me, puzzled.

"Why are you giving me those?"

"Go and visit the apartment, see whether it would suit you. That will save us some time. I've written down the address and the code for the front door. Third floor, left-hand side. As you'll see, there are three bedrooms. If you decide to take it, you can have the one with a separate entrance onto the landing, and the little connecting room, which you could use as a study. They both overlook the courtyard. The wallpaper was vile so I stripped it, but I never got round to repainting. It's just bare plaster, but you can put up posters. My room is on the other side of the hall, overlooking the boulevard, it has an en-suite bathroom. Here!"

He catches the keys, looking a little dazed.

"Do you usually give your keys to just anyone?"

"Why, are you just anyone?"

Battleship sunk.

T HE LITTLE MADAM is a lot thinner, I'll give her that. There's nothing like giving birth to lose weight.

She no longer looks like a barrel with legs. I wouldn't say she's stunning—she's a fourteen-year-old-girl, I can't bring myself to think of her as a woman, and besides, she's not pretty—but I have to admit that there's something different about her. A certain serenity, or a maturity, I'm not sure.

There is something different about her eyes, and that completely changes a face. Motherhood suits her, I think it's as simple as that.

She is sitting at the little table opposite the bed, tapping on the keyboard with that familiar rapt concentration. Sometimes she gives a little chuckle, probably a joke sent by one of her friends.

She has left the brat in her room, for which relief much thanks.

I wonder whether she wanted it, the kid, whether she really understood what having a baby meant, whether she loves the father?

Maëva suddenly bursts out laughing, then quickly claps her hands over her mouth and glances at me, blushing to the roots of her hair, and says "Sorry!" in a tone that sounds sincere, then dissolves into giggles so loud that if she tried to stop them, they would come out of her ears.

I smile in spite of myself.

She is laughing more quietly, typing frantically, then stops, reads, clucks like a guinea fowl and types another message. She sways to the bass rhythm leaking from her MP3 player.

She winds a lock of hair around her finger, bites her thumbnail, I can see her lips move as she reads the reply. Her tongue toys with the piercing in her bottom lip, which does nothing for her profile. But it is fascinating to watch from an anthropological viewpoint.

I look at the time, oops, nearly time for the news…

A young mother needs limits if she is to keep to her busy schedule, surely?

I attempt a subtle ruse:

"You don't think maybe the baby will be getting hungry?"

She glances at the clock at the bottom of the screen, shrugs and, without turning, she says.

"Yeah, you're right, I'd better get going."

I assume she is saying goodbye to her friends, it takes a while for her to type the words.

She comes over and sets the laptop down on the nightstand, her eyes still twinkling with laughter.

"What's the father's name?"

"Huh?"

"The baby's father, do you know his name?"

From her devastated look, I wonder whether she realizes that all babies have a father by default. Has she understood the cause and effect between the cake mix and the bun in the oven?

"Of course I know," she snaps irritably. "His name's Lucas."

"Is he your boyfriend?"

She rolls her eyes and says in a condescending tone:

"He's not my 'boyfriend', he's just a friend. Jeez."

"And… um… is he happy about being a dad, this friend of yours?"

She gives a smile so big I can see her molars.

"Yeah, he's dead proud, obvs. I sent him the photos you took this morning."

Well, that's something.

"So… he's fourteen too?"

She opens her eyes wide as dinner plates. I can tell she just about manages not to say, "Are you stupid, or what?"

"No way… He's, like, twenty… well, nearly."

I'm betting that this Lucas who is "nearly" twenty is not much more mature than she is.

Suddenly, I think I hear Camille's voice, "You just can't stop yourself judging other people, can you?" I put a lid on my prejudices and a tourniquet to staunch the flow of convictions. Keep on thinking like an old duffer, and you end up becoming one.

Since the little shrew has willingly submitted to my inter-rogation, I make the most of it to ask the question that has been on the tip of my tongue.

"Did… did you really want it, this baby? I'm mean, you're still very young."

"Yeah, but at least this way I'll be able to leave home."

"Oh? Were things really that bad at home?"

"Too right, I was never allowed to do *anything*. But I'm pretty hacked off being stuck in here. It's been, like, a month. Enough already."

"A month?"

She wedges her chewing gum into her cheek, sniffles, shrugs.

"Yeah, the doctor wanted to keep me in, on account of the baby's head not being engaged, and its weight, that kind of thing. But it's all fine now, it's done, in three days I'll be out of here."

The prospect of some peace and quiet is thrilling. Three days.

It can't come soon enough…

Maëva carries on, she has never been so talkative.

"We're gonna get married, me and Lucas, that way I'll legally be a grown-up. And then I can do whatever I like, I'll be free, it's awesome."

Free, with a kid on your hands? The jury's out on that one…

T ELEPHONES IN HOSPITALS are installed according to strict scientific principles based on two key criteria: distance from bed should be just far enough to make it impossible to pick up on the first ring, and volume of the aforesaid ring should be just loud enough to cause tinnitus.

I manage to answer on the fifth attempt.

I instantly recognize the voice of my old friend Serge.

"Bloody hell, you're a hard man to get hold of," he roars. "Every time I phone, they tell me you're with the physio or having more X-rays. Be careful, or you'll end up glowing in the dark."

"What's up? When did you get back from holidays?"

"Couple of days ago, I haven't been able to call until now."

"How are things?"

"I'd love to say 'great', but let's be honest: fair to middling."

"Why, what's up?"

"My cardiologist isn't happy with me. He says I've got palpitations off the Richter scale. Claims it's the cigarettes, though personally I blame the kouign-amann. I think I might have consumed a lethal dose."

I know Serge, the worse things are, the more he jokes about it.

"What does he suggest you do?"

"Have myself carved up like a chicken so they can splice the tubing back together. He calls it a triple-bypass, I call it butchery."

"When is the op?"

"I go under the knife Monday next."

"Oh?"

"Affirmative! Apparently, I don't have my whole life to fart around making a decision…"

"So, you're going to be admitted just as I'm finally getting discharged."

"Yeah, hospital policy apparently, two old fools is one too many."

He cracks up, I do too.

We might as well laugh, we're still alive.

"SHE'S A REAL CASE, that girl of yours."

Myriam chatters away as usual while she conducts her examination. I think in my case it's just routine now, there's no real cause for concern, but she remains conscientious. She checks my blood pressure, sticks a thermometer in my right ear and takes my temperature.

Ever since I arrived, I've felt like battered old jalopy in the hands of obsessive car mechanics. Oil check, tyre pressure, 67,000-km service.

Any moment now, I figure someone will pop open my bonnet.

"What do you mean, 'a real case'?"

"From what I heard, she's been in care for the past year."

"Really? She told me that 'at home' she's never allowed to do anything."

"Oh, she hasn't lived 'at home' for an age! One of the youth workers was chatting with one of my colleagues. They go to the same gym."

"And?…"

"Her father's inside, he's been banged up for a few months for GBH, he was involved in a knife fight, someone

was seriously hurt. Could you move your leg a little?...
There, that's perfect. The scars are healing well, with a bit
of luck, after a while they won't even be visible... What
was I saying?"

"The girl..."

"Oh, yes. Anyway, apparently she and her mother didn't
get along at all, they fought all the time. When the father
ended up in prison, the girl left home, lived on the streets
for a few weeks, got herself arrested for shoplifting. She
wasn't even thirteen!"

"Hmm... not exactly an auspicious start to life."

"No shit Sherlock. Anyway, the police took her back to
her mother, but she just kept running away, five or six times
she scarpered, eventually they had to put her in a home
since she doesn't have any other family. That's where she
met the boyfriend."

"Oh, right. So he's in care too?"

"No, not at all, he's a cook, works in the kitchens. The
social worker says the two of them are genuinely in love.
The guy is very responsible. He's level-headed."

I crack up laughing.

"You've got a very strange concept of what it means to
be responsible! A guy pushing twenty who gets a thirteen-
year-old pregnant has a long way to go when it comes to
being 'level-headed', don't you think?"

Myriam laughs and nods vigorously as she removes the
last of the bandages.

"Yeah, but he's in love. It seems that he's really happy

about the baby. You know, in a situation like this, a lot of lads would be long gone. For a man, a baby is a real commitment, trust me."

I'm sure this is true, although personally I have no experience.

"IT WASN'T EXACTLY sensible to give him the keys, if you want my opinion."

"I'm not a suspicious person, my friend."

"Well I am. Occupational hazard. He seems like a decent guy, I'm not saying otherwise. But the courts and the police stations are full of young thugs with angelic faces."

"You have a very dim view of lawyers and cops, don't you?" Maxime laughs.

"You just can't turn it off, can you? No, but seriously, you know nothing about this boy, aside from the fact that he turns tricks. It's hardly a testament to his moral probity."

"What have I got to lose, apart from a huge TV that's at least fifteen years old? I'm convinced he's a decent kid."

"You're only saying that because he fished you out of the Seine."

"Well… the fact that he saved my life is a point in his favour, I can't deny it."

"OK, I won't say any more. In any case, we've got his details on file, if there are any problems it won't be hard to track him down. I just hope you're not in for a nasty surprise."

"Let me tell you something: if you spend your life trying to avoid 'nasty surprises', you miss out on the good ones too."

He smiles.

"You're right. Sometimes, I can be a grumpy old git…"

"Don't be so presumptuous: I'm the grumpy old git here. You'll have to make do with being a tetchy young bastard. No need to get ahead of yourself. All things come to those who wait, take my word for it…"

"RIGHT, I'M OUTTA HERE, so I just popped in to say goodbye, yeah?"

She is wearing a denim skirt not much bigger than a belt, a pair of tights that look like the nets from a fishing trawler, and a jumper baggy enough to contain her breasts.

She's chewing gum, as always, she sways her hips to the *boom chaka boom!* seeping from her headphones, and maybe it's her way of putting a brave face on things.

"Is your boyfriend coming to fetch you?"

"Yeah, in about an hour. But don't get me wrong, he's not…"

"… your boyfriend, I know."

She tugs at a lock of hair, rubs her nose with the back of her hand and asks:

"Any chance I can go on Facebook, just for a sec?"

"Be my guest."

She is shocked. Usually, I say "no", not that she pays me any mind. Me giving her permission catches her off guard.

"Call it a leaving present," I say.

She smiles, picks the laptop, sashays over to the little table, slumps into the chair. I can see her tinkering with something.

"What are you up to?"

"I'm just uploading photos for some of my girlfriends."

Pictures of her love child, I presume.

I make a display of great forbearance, after all she'll be gone for good by tonight and, besides, I'm reading a Ken Follett that has had me hooked from the first page. I'm grateful to the young cop for lending it to me. I'm lucky enough to be a very slow reader, so a thousand-page book is the equivalent of days of solitary pleasure.

In return, I've promised Maxime that as soon as I get out, I'll take him for dinner to 'Le Chapon Déluré', a little restaurant on the banks of the Seine I'm very fond of, where they commit crimes involving duck *confit* and truffles and *foie gras* that would lead anyone with taste buds to sell his grandmother.

He said:

"No, no, there's no need to thank me. When exactly did you have in mind?"

I'm betting that we'll set a date soon; the consultant no longer comes to bother me, which I have to assume is a good sign.

With two fingers, the little madam types out her memoirs on Facebook. This is her drug.

I set up an account to see what it's all about. You have to be very young, very lonely, or very, very bored to go around *friending* people, most of whom you barely know, people you got along happily without before you had a Facebook account, the sort of people you wouldn't last ten minutes with under normal circumstances.

*

Right, Maëva has finished sharing her photos, she gets up.

"Don't turn it off, please, I need to check my email."

"OK, no sweat."

With all the care of a nanny, she sets the laptop on the nightstand.

"I'll be leaving after lunch."

"I suppose you're happy?"

"Yeah, it's wicked. I can't wait…"

"This name you chose, Justin…"

I do my best to pronounce it as she does, with an American accent.

"… you never told me what it means. I assume you know?"

She grins, giving me a clear view of the slobbery chewing gum she has just wedged between two premolars.

"Yeah. It means 'reasonable'…"

"Let's hope it suits him, then."

She laughs.

"Right, well…"

She's just like my brother.

She squirms, not knowing how to say goodbye to me. Eventually she mutters:

"… I'll be off, then."

"You do that. Travel safely. And don't forget to buy our own laptop."

She giggles, and wavers for a moment.

"I hope they'll let you out soon… and that… things will be OK."

I give her a wink.

"Don't you worry about me, I'm a hard nut to crack, I've seen worse."

She nods, gives me a little wave, and walks out of the room and out of my life.

Forgetting to close the door.

I'm going to write a little note to Serge, who must be pretty freaked out. It would take a lot less to depress most people.

The little madam has left her Facebook page open. Her "wall", as the converts to this new sect refer to it. It is filled with asinine messages—so full of mistakes they are almost poetic—and photographs of young people pulling faces, making rabbit ears behind their friends' heads. Nothing new in the world of drunken teenagers.

Being curious, I take a look at her photographs, since there is no expectation of privacy.

I get to see the father, the famous Lucas who is "nearly twenty". A chubby lad with a cheerful face, he looks honest, down-to-earth, a simple soul. The sort of person you could look at in his pram and know what he will look like when he is fifty-five. There is a series of photos of him with the little madam as she starts to balloon, at a funfair, in a café, standing on a flight of steps, surrounded by friends. The exhibition is annotated: *Doudou and me at the fun fair; Magali's B-day bash, great laugh; Doudou and me, 1 yr annaversay!*

From the way they stand, the way they hold each other, it is obvious that they are in love, even if he is not her *boyfriend*.

Then there are three photographs taken in this very room.

Two of the ones I took of the new mother and her baba. The caption reads *My little bundellof joy*. And one of me with the baby in my arms. Me as a grumpy old git, a misanthropic, badly shaven old codger. Me, cradling in my feeble arms, the little madam's little sprog.

And underneath, the caption: *Justin with his granddad Jean-Piere*.

Note, she only put one 'R' in Pierre.

Though that's hardly a good enough reason for me to feel so emotional.

I AM IN THE MIDDLE of getting dressed. The door flies open, then the nursing auxiliary knocks.

She scuttles in sideways, like a figure in an Egyptian frieze, still facing out into the corridor as she finishes the sentence addressed to someone else. I hear her colleague laughing.

The nurse coming in calls back "You should have seen the face on him!" then, without pausing for breath, still giggling, she calls to me in a sing-song voice:

"*Morrrr*-ning! This was left at reception for you!"

I eventually win the battle with my trousers, all the while politely responding to the greetings of everyone passing in the hallway.

In the envelope are my keys.

Camille clearly did not think it necessary to return them personally. I see it as a casual way of saying go to hell. And it makes me livid.

Why do we feel so personally rejected when our gifts are not appreciated? It is as though we spend our whole lives like kids in nursery school, looking into our mothers' eyes to see her marvel at our pasta necklaces.

*

I immediately come up with reasons why I don't give a toss: I'll be happier on my own in the apartment, without having some kid under my feet. He seems nice enough, but you can tell he's stubborn. He would probably have spent all day listening to rap, and I can't abide rap.

I offered my help. If he doesn't want it, the little bastard can go to hell!

I only suggested it as a favour to him.

It's not as though I need anything, I certainly don't need any help. I'll find someone else to do my shopping. I'm old enough and ugly enough to get along by myself.

I'm not completely disabled.

See? I managed to put on my trousers all by myself in less than ten minutes… and I'm as happy as a four-year-old who's just managed to put his gloves on for the first time.

Sometimes I depress myself.

Head held high, crutch at the ready, I head downstairs to the cafeteria for a little break. In the lift, a woman of a certain age—by which I mean much younger that me—stares at me, at my package, with a tact that does not escape me.

I smile, she turns away. I respect her confusion.

I emerge from the lift, go into the cafeteria, order a coffee and stand, looking out of the picture window, a vague smile playing on my lips.

A passing orderly stops and whispers to me.

"Your flies are undone."

THE UROLOGIST stops by briefly, running late as always. We haven't seen each other in a while, him and me.

He takes a last look through my patient file, asks two or three quick questions and, having been assured that I piss just like I used to do, declares in a breezy tone:

"Well, from my point of view, you're fine!"

The turn of phrase is curious, but logical. Whatever fellow-feeling he may have, he nonetheless sees me within a carefully delimited context: bladder, dick, urethra.

The orthopaedist looks after the woodwork, the neurologist takes care of the wiring.

My urologist deals with the drains.

Never talk to your tiler about plumbing, therein lie the beginnings of wisdom.

Specialists are as short-sighted as moles, they view their patients only in close-up and see them only in terms of what's right under their nose.

A sad life for a proctologist.

"ARE WE OFF SOON?"

"Yes, and 'we' are very happy to be leaving, I can tell you."

The ward assistant has come to take away the breakfast tray. She stands in front of the bed, hands on the small of her back, and bends backwards—obviously a long-time lumbago sufferer. She sighs and then says cheerfully:

"After all this time, I'm sure there are people pining for you at home, hmm?"

"Not really, I live alone."

She looks at me sadly. She cannot believe her ears.

"All on your own? No family, no children?"

"Nope. Just me."

She babbles on, incredulous:

"Not even a dog or a cat?"

I can tell that to her I represent the subterranean depths of human misery.

No children, no dog, no cat.

Oh shit, the cat!

I suddenly remember.

That damned grey moggie with half-chewed ears that moved into my apartment, with its array of irritating habits:

purring, head-butting my chin, kneading my belly with its paws. I found it outside the building a couple of months ago, skinny as a rake. I don't know why I let it follow me upstairs. Maybe something about the way it said *Mrrrrraouw*? No sooner was in the apartment than it devoured my tinned sardines with gusto and polished off my lamb and bean stew—beans and all, which I found surprising. He made a thoughtful tour of the property. Eventually, he picked on *my* spot on the sofa and started to throw up, head down, perfectly concentrated.

This set me thinking and I realized I didn't want to be burdened with looking after a pet—oh, no!—I had gone sixty-seven years without, there was no need to start now. I put my words into action, I opened the apartment door, and *hup!*

But the cat was not prepared to accept my decision, for two hours he sat on the welcome mat, serenading me with a growl like a tiger. I took him downstairs and put him outside. He waited until one of my neighbours opened the front door then darted upstairs, parked himself outside my door and started yowling again. I gave in.

I kept the beast, I called him Dishrag.

I thought we had a lot in common: forever grumpy, always complaining, never satisfied.

It was because of him I was on the bridge the night of the accident, I remember it now.

*

This moggy was as clingy as a lovelorn teenager, he followed me everywhere, I had to be careful every time I left the apartment to make sure he did not come with me.

That night, I took the bins out at about one o'clock, just before I went to bed. I always forget until the last minute. I didn't notice he had followed me, and when I finally did notice, it was because he was being attacked by a huge dog. I threw the dustbin at the cur, much to his master's annoyance; but the damage was done, Dishrag was badly injured.

The dog's owner was pretty decent. Since he was parked nearby, he offered to drive me to the nearest vet. There are not many duty vets on Sunday and Monday nights. I must have made a dozen phone calls and got eleven answering machines. Eventually, I managed to find one who was not too far from my place—a stroke of luck—though I can't remember the name or the address. The dog owner took me in his car under the glowering eye of his dog, who would happily have bitten my leg off and then finished off Dishrag, who was already dying from a gaping wound in his belly.

I seem to remember the vet being young, and I have a vague memory of hanging around in the waiting room for hours, then heading home on foot, without my cat.

So, that night, I was coming back from the vet.

If it were not for that bloody cat, I would not have crossed that bridge, or sailed over the parapet, and I would not have been stitched back together like a tattered pair of overalls.

This is what happens when you're kind to animals.

Mystery solved.

Except for the fact that I don't know what became of my feline friend.

Tonight, there was an email from Nathalie, Serge's girlfriend.

As promised, she wrote to give me a brief update, the operation was this morning, it went as well as could be expected, but it is still too early to tell.

Serge had put off going to his doctor. Apparently he had needed the operation for some time. He will need a lot of rest.

She will keep me posted.

Before the operation, he asked her to pass on a message to me, which she copy-pasted at the bottom of her email.

Hello my friend,

A joyous collection of quotes before I head off to be sliced up (tomorrow morning, Jesus I'm scared shitless):

"I'd rather die covered in blood than an old man lying in my own piss."—Randall Wallace

"To depart is to die a little, but to die is to depart a lot."—Alphonse Allais

"Medicine makes it possible to die more slowly"—Plutarch

And, for dessert:

"Good health is a precarious state which presages nothing good."—Jules Romains

We'll talk about this over a goose *confit*, but for the time being I remain

Serge

I reply to Nathalie—whom I have never met—and attach a message to pass on to Serge when he is able to read:

Hello my friend,

In response to the final quotation from your optimistic anthology, here is another thought that I find quite uplifting:

"Health is what prevents you from dying every time you are seriously ill." Georges Perros

Keep well, my friend.

They're discharging me on Wednesday, I'll wait to hear from you.

I'm up for the goose *confit*, but I'll cook it.

Much love,

Pierrot

"My young friend, they are letting me out on Wednesday, I hope you've worked up an appetite, we'll soon be having dinner at 'Le Chapon Déluré!'"

"I've been preparing—I haven't eaten a thing for three days."

"I'm afraid that might not be enough. Try to persevere a little longer."

"Don't worry, I'm nothing if not persistent. Do you need any help getting home on Wednesday? Depending on what time you're discharged, I might be able to drive you—let me know, you've got my mobile number."

"A police escort back to my apartment after an unexplained six-week absence?... I have to say I'm tempted, if only to see the look on my neighbours' faces..."

"I can even crank up the lights and sirens as we pull up in front of the building if you like."

"Now that would be asking too much. No, don't worry about it, I'll take a taxi."

I give him back the Ken Follett and offer to lend him an Umberto Eco he hasn't read yet.

I say:

"The kid gave back the keys."

"Oh? So, is he going to crash at your place? What did he say?"

"Absolutely nothing, he left them in an envelope at reception."

"Really?"

"Really."

"It's probably for the best, you know. I mean, it was nice of you to offer but... well, a bit risky. You don't owe the boy anything."

"Except my life. Though, given how much of it is left, I suppose it's not a great debt."

Maxime laughs, the idiot.

He gestures to a plastic bag he put on the table opposite my bed when he came in.

"You have a DVD player I assume?"

"Of course! Incredible as it might seem, such cutting-edge technology has made it all the way to people like me."

"I brought you a few films, you can give them back when we go for dinner, or whenever. You'll see, they're amazing!"

In return I promise to lend him a collection of classic American movies from the '40s, which he *could* watch with subtitles if absolutely necessary.

He takes his leave, we say our goodbyes.

The tray arrives with lunch, braised chicory and ham, green beans, plain yoghurt.

At last, being in hospital has made me feel young again: if I closed my eyes, I might think I was in summer camp.

"SO, YOU'RE ABANDONING US?"

"Yes, I'm leaving at two o'clock. In your case, of course, parting is such sweet sorrow, my aurora borealis!"

"You think I believe that? Go on, you'll be much better off at home."

Myriam dips into the box of chocolates I had Maxime buy for her. Yummm, she says, blissfully content, her eyes closed, then winks and proffers the box towards me, as though she were suggesting a quickie.

Might as well face facts, most women don't need us: a box of chocolates is a more than adequate substitute for an orgasm.

I take a chocolate. She approves of my choice as an informed amateur.

"Thank you, I mean that. It's very sweet. It's not every day we get gifts from patients, you know. Is someone coming to pick you up later?"

"No, I'll take a taxi."

"You did remember to make an appointment to see your physio, didn't you?"

I inform her that I have a schedule as packed as a junior minister: physio, swimming, out-patient appointments with the consultant, follow-up X-rays three months from now…

"I'm going to miss you, I don't get many like you in this place. Come here, give me a kiss!"

She warps her arms around me and plants a warm, sincere smacker on my cheek, I feel suddenly touched. Just my luck—I'm starting to get soppy.

We are born a reed, we become an oak, we end up balsa wood.

THE PHONE RINGS. It is Maxime.

"Ah, I was afraid you might have left already. Sorry I didn't have time to swing by the hospital, but I just wanted to let you know I've concluded that little investigation."

"Really? Already?"

"You've either got what it takes to be an exceptional cop, or you haven't…"

"So?"

"So, his name is Delaroche, he is based at 38 rue des Grèves which, as you said, isn't far from your place. He managed to save the cat, but when you didn't come back to collect it, he gave it to a local refuge. 'Little Kitties' on the boulevard Magenta. The cat is still there, if you want it."

"Are you kidding? Weeks, I've spent in hospital being poked and prodded and fed plain yoghurt, I'm going to need a walking stick for months, not to mention the hours of physio… Given what he's cost me, I'm not going to let that furbag go to someone else."

"Wait, we're not done yet, you're going to get a bill from the vet, he managed to wheedle your address out of me. Given the fee, I'm hoping for your sake that it's a pedigree."

"He's pure-blood alley of good sewer stock, I'll have you know. You'll see for yourself when you pick me up to take me to the restaurant."

"I'm looking forward to meeting him! What's his name, Kitty? Precious? Smokey?"

"Dishrag."

"Not bad, not bad. I named my dog Toerag. Right, got to go, I've got work."

"And I should go downstairs and wait for my taxi."

I SNAP SHUT the suitcase, take a last look at the room.
Can't say I haven't met anyone.

A fourteen-year old mother, a rent boy studying for a degree, a sentimental cop in search of a father, a churlish consultant, a philosophical nurse, an optimistic physiotherapist, a depressive neurologist, an overworked urologist, day nurses, night nurses, harried nurses' aides and unhurried orderlies, a student nurse.

Like a poem by Prévert.

THE WEATHER IS SHIT, the taxi smells of wet dog and the lobby of my building is cold as the grave.

As I struggle to climb the stairs, I realize there is probably nothing to eat in the house, and I don't have the energy to totter as far as the corner shop on my crutches. Third floor, no lift, one gammy leg, I can tell this isn't going to be fun.

The apartment is in darkness, the curtains are drawn. Camille must have closed them when he came to visit, or maybe it was my brother. I usually leave them open.

I lurch as far as the kitchen. I'm thirsty. A little beer?

As I expected, the fridge is full of cold air whistling through the empty shelves. Two mouldering tomatoes, half a chicken desiccated as a mummy, some rancid butter, a few yoghurts past their sell-by date and three cans of beer.

The cupboards are not much more welcoming: crackers, coffee, pasta, lentils, Dishrag's cans of sardines, two stock cubes fighting a duel, a bottle of ketchup and a packet of crisps. Enough to withstand a siege for at least a week. All I'm missing is a phial of arsenic, or a tin of rat poison.

I go into the living room and throw open the curtains.

On the table, there is a bottle of decent white wine. Under the bottle is a page from a loose-leaf binder. A laconic message:

You pay for the paint, I'll decorate the room. What do you say to white?
    Camille.

White? Don't mind if I do.
    I'll pour myself a little glass.

PUSHKIN PRESS

Pushkin Press was founded in 1997, and publishes novels, essays, memoirs, children's books—everything from timeless classics to the urgent and contemporary.

Our books represent exciting, high-quality writing from around the world: we publish some of the twentieth century's most widely acclaimed, brilliant authors such as Stefan Zweig, Marcel Aymé, Teffi, Antal Szerb, Gaito Gazdanov and Yasushi Inoue, as well as compelling and award-winning contemporary writers, including Andrés Neuman, Edith Pearlman, Eka Kurniawan and Ayelet Gundar-Goshen.

Pushkin Press publishes the world's best stories, to be read and read again. Here are just some of the titles from our long and varied list. To discover more, visit www.pushkinpress.com.

THE SPECTRE OF ALEXANDER WOLF
GAITO GAZDANOV

'A mesmerising work of literature' Antony Beevor

SUMMER BEFORE THE DARK
VOLKER WEIDERMANN

'For such a slim book to convey with such poignancy the extinction of a generation of "Great Europeans" is a triumph' *Sunday Telegraph*

MESSAGES FROM A LOST WORLD
STEFAN ZWEIG

'At a time of monetary crisis and political disorder... Zweig's celebration of the brotherhood of peoples reminds us that there is another way' *The Nation*

BINOCULAR VISION
EDITH PEARLMAN

'A genius of the short story' Mark Lawson, *Guardian*

IN THE BEGINNING WAS THE SEA
TOMÁS GONZÁLEZ

'Smoothly intriguing narrative, with its touches of sinister, Patricia Highsmith-like menace' *Irish Times*

BEWARE OF PITY
STEFAN ZWEIG

'Zweig's fictional masterpiece' *Guardian*

THE ENCOUNTER
PETRU POPESCU

'A book that suggests new ways of looking at the world and our place within it' *Sunday Telegraph*

WAKE UP, SIR!
JONATHAN AMES

'The novel is extremely funny but it is also sad and poignant, and almost incredibly clever' *Guardian*

THE WORLD OF YESTERDAY
STEFAN ZWEIG

'*The World of Yesterday* is one of the greatest memoirs of the twentieth century, as perfect in its evocation of the world Zweig loved, as it is in its portrayal of how that world was destroyed' David Hare

WAKING LIONS
AYELET GUNDAR-GOSHEN

'A literary thriller that is used as a vehicle to explore big moral issues. I loved everything about it' *Daily Mail*

BONITA AVENUE
PETER BUWALDA

'One wild ride: a swirling helix of a family saga… a new writer as toe-curling as early Roth, as roomy as Franzen and as caustic as Houellebecq' *Sunday Telegraph*

JOURNEY BY MOONLIGHT
ANTAL SZERB

'Just divine… makes you imagine the author has had private access to your own soul' Nicholas Lezard, *Guardian*

BEFORE THE FEAST

SAŠA STANIŠIĆ

'Exceptional… cleverly done, and so mesmerising from
the off… thought-provoking and energetic' *Big Issue*

A SIMPLE STORY

LEILA GUERRIERO

'An epic of noble proportions… [Guerriero] is a mistress
of the telling phrase or the revealing detail' *Spectator*

FORTUNES OF FRANCE

ROBERT MERLE

1 *The Brethren*

2 *City of Wisdom and Blood*

3 *Heretic Dawn*

'Swashbuckling historical fiction' *Guardian*

TRAVELLER OF THE CENTURY

ANDRÉS NEUMAN

'A beautiful, accomplished novel: as ambitious as it is generous,
as moving as it is smart' Juan Gabriel Vásquez, *Guardian*

ONE NIGHT, MARKOVITCH

AYELET GUNDAR-GOSHEN

'Wry, ironically tinged and poignant… this is a fable
for the twenty-first century' *Sunday Telegraph*

KARATE CHOP & MINNA NEEDS REHEARSAL SPACE

DORTHE NORS

'Unique in form and effect… Nors has found a novel
way of getting into the human heart' *Guardian*

RED LOVE: THE STORY OF AN EAST GERMAN FAMILY

MAXIM LEO

'Beautiful and supremely touching… an unbearably poignant
description of a world that no longer exists' *Sunday Telegraph*

SONG FOR AN APPROACHING STORM

PETER FRÖBERG IDLING

'Beautifully evocative… a must-read novel' *Daily Mail*

THE RABBIT BACK LITERATURE SOCIETY
PASI ILMARI JÄÄSKELÄINEN

'Wonderfully knotty... a very grown-up fantasy masquerading as quirky fable. Unexpected, thrilling and absurd' *Sunday Telegraph*

STAMMERED SONGBOOK: A MOTHER'S BOOK OF HOURS
ERWIN MORTIER

'Mortier has a poet's eye for vibrant detail and prose to match... If this is a book of fragmentation, it is also a son's moving tribute' *Observer*

BARCELONA SHADOWS
MARC PASTOR

'As gruesome as it is gripping... the writing is extraordinarily vivid... Highly recommended' *Independent*

THE LIBRARIAN
MIKHAIL ELIZAROV

'A romping good tale... Pretty sensational' *Big Issue*

WHILE THE GODS WERE SLEEPING
ERWIN MORTIER

'A monumental, phenomenal book' *De Morgen*

BUTTERFLIES IN NOVEMBER
AUÐUR AVA ÓLAFSDÓTTIR

'A funny, moving and occasionally bizarre exploration of life's upheavals and reversals' *Financial Times*

BY BLOOD
ELLEN ULLMAN

'Delicious and intriguing' *Daily Telegraph*

THE LAST DAYS
LAURENT SEKSIK

'Mesmerising... Seksik's portrait of Zweig's final months is dignified and tender' *Financial Times*

TALKING TO OURSELVES
ANDRÉS NEUMAN

'This is writing of a quality rarely encountered... when you read Neuman's beautiful novel, you realise a very high bar has been set' *Guardian*